ISBN 978-1-7356456-0-5

First edition: September 2020

Book design by Adam Hay Studio

www.mohalipress.com

www.aishalelouma.com
Twitter @aishalelouma
Facebook.com/aisha-lelouma
Instagram.com/aishalelouma

To Be Amina

A Novel

Aisha Lelouma Diallo

Mohali Press

Chapter One

"You are a lamp in the darkness," my mother said to me. We were sitting on our terrace in the back of our house in Simbaya, and she was gently stroking my newly done braids.

"Neneh, why are you going to Kamsar?" I asked.

"Because I have to get better, ma chérie. Neneh is not feeling well, and she has to go see the doctor in Kamsar."

"When are you coming back?"

"Soon, bobo, soon." She beamed down at me.

"Neneh, I will get you your own doctor when I grow

up so you won't have to go anywhere," I said, trying to comfort her. She had been ill for a few days and barely had the energy to prop herself up in bed earlier that day.

"God willing, that would be wonderful," she said and gave me a gentle hug.

That was the last conversation I had with my mother and little did I know that it also marked one of my last days as an ordinary child. I was eight years old.

She left shortly after with my Uncle Bachir, and she waved at me through the passenger seat window, a faint smile on her face.

Every time after that, whenever I have let my mind wander back to that afternoon on that terrace, and once I have gotten past the tightness in my throat, I can almost feel my mother's hand on the back of my head. I have been uncertain of how I've managed to remember the details of that day—from the soft breeze that slowly moved the leaves of the mango tree in the yard, to the dim voices carried over to us every time the wind got a little stronger, to the smell of the Karité oil that my mother had applied to my hair to loosen the tightness in my braids—but it would all be very clear, as if it were happening again right before my eyes. I could see myself there. I could feel myself there.

I looked out of the corner of my eye and saw Mr. Bah quietly walking up and down the narrow lane that separated the boys' section from the girls' in our classroom as he clearly enunciated the words he was dictating to us. It was hot and stuffy in the room. The metal shutters had been closed to keep the sun out, but it also kept the air from flowing, and despite the effort, the rays of the sun still found their way in, piercing through the holes in the sheet metal and landing like halos on the cement ground and the wooden desks. I glanced at the ancient pendulum on the wall, hoping it was getting closer to break time. We always had our break from noon to two o'clock, and most students went home for lunch, except for the children who lived too far away. They usually bought food from the lady right outside the school gate, or they sometimes tagged along with a friend. My friends Fatima, Mamady, Oumi, and I took turns eating at each other's houses, and we would talk and drool about what was stewing in the pots back at our houses long before lunchtime. After lunch, we would then head back and play in the school's courtyard until we heard the bell that prompted us to head back to our desks. The "bell" was actually an old wheelbase that the custodian thumped with a heavy piece of metal at precise times that marked the start and end of class time, with recess in between. If the sound of the bell resonated at any other time than the specified ones, we were all to convene around the flagpole, where special announcements were made. It was also where we sang our national anthem at the beginning and the end of each day. The school day did not officially start until the flag was flying high on the pole and our barely awake voices had intoned "Liberté"; and of course, the school day wasn't over until the flag was carefully lowered to the sound of our voices and neatly folded and placed on Mr. Keita's desk.

As Mr. Bah dictated, he suddenly stopped and loudly said "Debout!" to prompt us onto our feet. We had to stand up every time Mr. Keita, the school director, came into the classroom or anytime we had some important visitors. I peeked behind me as I was standing up and saw Mr. Keita in the doorway; something was quite peculiar. It was not unusual for the director to drop in to give us pop oral quizzes or just observe us as we were all on pins and needles trying to give the correct answers to the questions posed by our teacher; but that day, something about his demeanor and the way he looked straight at me while walking up the aisle was very strange. I was overcome by a feeling of panic when he stood right in front of me. My mind started racing. Was I in trouble? What could I have done that was so terrible, that Mr. Keita would pay me a visit during class time? I rarely got into trouble at school, and I was actually quite the studious pupil. My mother never failed to remind me of how lucky I was to attend school, a private school for that matter, while most little girls my age headed to the local market every morning to help their mothers sell vegetables. The only time my parents were called over to meet the director was that one time when I let

Mamady convince me to go to town during geography class. The French cultural center had just received a new shipment of books, and we had to be there first to pick the best books. He persuaded me that we would be back before long and that no one would even notice we were missing from class. The comfy air-conditioned room and the smell of the books must have carried us away, because three hours later, we both jumped up from the sound of a book being thrown on the floor and realized our gaffe. Not too much later after returning to school, we were escorted to the director's office.

"Pick up your books and come with me." Mr. Keita's voice brought me out of my daze. His voice, which was usually stern, had a slight glint of compassion, or had I imagined it in the hope that I wouldn't be reprimanded too harshly for whatever I had done? I collected my books and put them in my bag in an orderly fashion. As I made my way to the door, I could hear whispers coming from all corners of the room. Mr. Keita gently put his hand on my shoulder. I maybe had not imagined the intonation in his voice after all, but why was he being suddenly so kind? My thoughts were interrupted by the sight of our family maid standing right outside in the school courtyard. Why was Bailao here? I had been walking myself to and from school for a few months, and the only time Bailao was sent to get me was when it was raining. The stream of the small river I had to cross on my way to school turned into a torrent every time it rained, and it was impossible for a child to cross without the help of an adult; but there were no clouds in sight—in fact, the skies were very clear, and the rays of the sun that had been doggedly piercing through the classroom shutters were blinding Bailao who was holding her hand up to shield her eyes. She started walking toward us, and as she approached, Mr. Keita slightly tapped my shoulder, and said: "She was sent to pick you up. You are excused for the rest of the day."

"But why?" I asked, and quickly added, "So, am I not in trouble?"

"No, you are not in trouble, and I believe this young lady will explain to you why she came for you. Go on now."

Bailao was now upon us. I looked up at her, and her eyes were red. I knew that her eyes only got red when she cried or when she had not gotten enough sleep after staying out late with her friends on the weekends.

"Mayin, Amina!" she said while extending her hand. I grabbed it and followed her. We walked in silence for a few minutes until I couldn't bear it anymore.

"Why have you come for me? The school day is not over yet, and it is not even raining."

"Your cousins Aziz and Habib are back."

My heart jumped. Aziz and Habib were my cousins from Paris. They had visited the previous summer, and it was the happiest summer I had ever had.

"Oh my god, Bailao, we have to walk faster. When did they arrive? Is Adama with them too?"

"Yes, they are all here," she answered me, but her voice was quivering.

"What is wrong, Bailao?" I asked, scrutinizing her face.

"Nothing."

"Then why are your eyes red?" I retorted, narrowing my eyes.

"Are they? Oh yes, that's right. I was grinding peppers earlier for the fish stew, and I accidentally rubbed my eyes before I washed my hands. That must be it."

I didn't believe her. Something in her voice was off, and she barely looked at me when she spoke, but I did not press her further. We walked for a moment before I blurted out, "Say, Bailao, why do you think my cousins are back so soon? It is not even summer. Don't they have school at this time in France?"

"I don't know. You ask too many questions!"

That was her way of saying that she did not wish to speak anymore, so silence fell again as we walked. I could feel the rocks on the road under my shoes. I noticed an old and rusty can of condensed milk on the side of the road, and I started kicking it as we continued on our way.

"Stop kicking the can!" Bailao said firmly. I reluctantly complied as I didn't want to get into trouble later, especially not with my cousins around.

I could see the final bend in the road that led to our house as we came up the hill. We lived in Simbaya Cité, a housing development built for the workers of a bauxite mining operation owned by a Russian firm. My father was an engineer, and my mother, an office administrator. I always proudly proclaimed my parents' work titles to anyone who asked, although I didn't really know what they meant. The fact that they were both employed by the mining company qualified them for a small villa in the development. Our house was a three-bedroom villa adorned with lush trees and two large terraces in the front and the back of the house. The home was air conditioned, which was a luxury, considering most households did not even have access to electricity. The water faucet on the side of the house served the neighborhood right outside the subdivision. They would come early in the morning carrying pails, large water cans, and all sorts of other containers to collect water for the day because the water they got from the well was not potable. The clinking sounds of metal pails and the voices of women talking were often how I knew it was dawn.

We were now on top of the hill, and I could see our home in the distance. I could also make out a grouping of people around the house.

"Who are all these people, Bailao?" I asked alarmingly.

She did not respond. Her face was very grave. I knew then that something was definitely wrong. I could sense it. I still wanted to believe that my cousins were at our house and that this was the reason why Bailao had come for me; but somehow, I knew that it wasn't the case. Something had not added up with the story all along. I felt a rapid anxiety building up inside me.

"Who are all these people, Bailao?" I repeated, this time my voice shaky and shrill. I could see people around the house, but I couldn't hear any of the sounds or noises that usually accompanied any large gathering of people. The only time when people in a large group were silent was when something bad had happened. I tried harder to persuade myself that everything was fine. When we got closer to the house, I saw my father sitting on the terrace, flanked on both sides by the neighborhood imam and our neighbor Mr. Fofana. The silence was deafening. As I walked up the stairs leading to the terrace, I heard a few murmurs. Bailao was no longer next to me; I looked around to see where she had gone, but all I met were unfamiliar faces apart from my mother's friends Mrs. Balde and Mrs. Sall. They were all quietly crying. What was happening? Something terrible had happened. Was Neneh back from Kamsar? Why wasn't she next to her friends? When I looked up, I felt my heart stop. The distressed look on my father's face was heartbreaking. I had never seen that expression on Baba's face.

"Baba!" I cried out as I ran toward him. "What is happening, Baba? Why are you so sad, Baba?"

My father looked at me but did not speak. His eyes were tearful, pained; and his lips trembled.

"Baba, why are you so sad?" I repeated. "Where is Neneh?"

Behind me, I heard someone snuffle. I felt myself being lifted from the ground, and when I turned my head, I realized that it was my Uncle Bachir picking me up. Why was everyone here but Neneh? Had something happened to my mother? She had been in Kamsar for a couple of weeks. She had promised me that she would be back soon.

"Kaou Bachir, where is my mother?" I asked again. Why isn't anyone answering me? Are they hearing me?

"I want my neneh!" I cried out, but again, it was met with silence, and a few sobs in the crowd.

My uncle carried me to the bedroom I shared with Bailao. My two brothers were sitting on the floor.

"Idrissa, keep an eye on your sister," he said as he sat me on the bed. He closed the door behind him when he walked out.

My older brother, Idrissa, was fifteen, and he attended the Lycée Sainte Marie, one of the best schools in the city. My paternal uncles made a fuss about Baba sending his Muslim son to a private Catholic school, but Baba just shrugged it off as backward thinking. Idrissa had to take a bus every day to go to school, and our parents always reminded him how much they were paying for his education and how important it was for him to set a good example for his little sister and brother. They told me one day that I would also take the required proficiency test to attend Sainte Marie as soon as I started middle school; and since then, I often imagined myself wearing the khaki uniform that the students at the school wore, proudly walking with my brother to the bus stop while passersby pointed and said, "Look at that little girl. She

13

goes to Sainte Marie; she must be very smart." I couldn't wait indeed.

I took one look at Idrissa slumped on the floor, and my stomach tied itself into a knot. My four-year-old younger brother, Ousmane, or Ousbi as we affectionately called him, sprang to his feet, started jumping in place, and excitedly shouted, "Neneh is dead! Neneh is dead!" as he giggled and threw himself on the bed.

"Shut up, Ousbi! You don't even know what that means!!" my brother shouted back as he stood up. My heart sank to my belly. I didn't think I truly knew the meaning of death, either, but what I did know for sure was that it was a place where people went and never came back.

"Dead? Koto Idrissa, is it true?" I looked at my older brother in fear.

"Yes," he said, his voice barely audible, his face constricted, staring forward but not looking at all.

"So, we will never see Neneh again?" I asked as my throat tightened. He stayed quiet this time and sat on the bed. He then abruptly said to me, "Don't cry! I heard that each tear you shed will burn through the skin of the deceased person you shed it for as soon as it hits the ground. We are not supposed to cry; we are supposed to accept that God took her back." Nothing of what he said made any sense to me, but I nevertheless compelled myself not to cry, which was almost impossible. My whole body was shaking as I tried to hold back the tears and emotions. I did not realize that I still had my backpack on, and my knuckles were almost pulsating from the grip I had on the straps. This couldn't be happening. It just couldn't.

My mother was buried that same day. Koto explained to me that she had to be buried as quickly as possible from the time of death to respect Islamic law. Her body was brought in a van from the morgue, where it had been washed and shrouded, then carried to the mosque for the funeral prayers before her burial. I did not see her body. I just caught a glimpse of the men carrying her, bundled in white sheets secured with ropes. They were taking away my neneh, almost running on the road that led to the cemetery. It was said that when someone died and they were destined for Heaven, their body weight became as light as a feather and the wind almost carried the men who transported the body to its last home. On the other hand, the bodies of people going to Hell became heavy, hard to carry, and weighted on the shoulders of its transporters. My neneh was going to Heaven.

Chapter Two

What happened subsequently was all a blur. People came and went for days. A procession of relatives, strangers, and friends all came to present their condolences. The kitchen and the dining room table were overflowing with dishes that mourners brought with them. The house was wrapped in a heavy silence; even Milou, our dog, was quiet as he rested every day on the first step leading to the terrace instead of running around the compound, wagging his tail and barking at passersby. Did Milou also know that Neneh was forever gone? At night, he moved from the steps to the front door. I thought about what Baba's mother, my nenehbaba, told us about dogs. Dogs guard the house against burglars, but most important, they guard us against evil spirits, unlike the devious cats, she would often say to us in her singing voice when we visited her in the village during the summer breaks. "But I love cats!" I would protest. She told us countless stories about the dog and the cat. I always remembered her favorite one. When evil spirits showed up at the door, she recounted, when the sky was dark as charcoal and the owners were sound asleep, the cat on guard duty lazily licked itself in the corner and left the door wide open for the nefarious night intruders to enter. The dog, on the other hand, jumped and blocked the door before asking:

"Who is there?"

"A friend," the evil spirit would answer.

"Friends do not visit when the sky is deep black," the dog would retort.

"I am a friend of your master; will you let me in?"

"All right, let me wake master first," the dog would answer, but the spirit would recoil and quickly say, "There is no need for that; it is a surprise."

"All right then," the dog would reply. "I will let you in, but first, you have to count all the hairs on my body." The evil spirit, afraid of the dog barking and waking its master, would be forced to start the wearisome task of counting the hairs in the dog's fur. The evil spirit tediously counted the hairs one by one, and just as it got close to the last strands, the dog would shake its whole body and fur as if it had just come out of the water. "Oh, I am sorry, Spirit, it is very ticklish when you are touching my hair, so I had to shake it off. Let's start over." The dog played this trick over and over until the rays of the sun started peeking out far in the east. Terrified to be found out, the evil spirit took off in a cloud of dust, hoping to never find that darned dog at the door again.

I wished Nenehbaba was there to hold me, comfort me, sing her songs to me, tuck me under her heavy, orange tiger blanket, and tell me that it was all a lie, that my neneh would be back home soon; but she was now too old to travel from the village to the city. I did not know my nenehkaou. She died in childbirth delivering Neneh's youngest sibling, Uncle Bachir. Both of my babaensoros had gone to war and never came back. They were pulled into their colonial masters' conflicts and lost their lives without understanding why. Nenehbaba told us how the French had come to the village one day, rounded up all the young men and the village chief, told them that the Germans had attacked them, and that therefore the Germans had also attacked their village. The French said these young men needed to fight alongside the white men to defend their community and prove to the Germans that Africans are human beings just like them, so off went all the young men, leaving behind wives and children. Few made it back. Baba often lamented that they had fought a war that was not theirs, and despite all the lives lost, the African soldiers' contribution in World War II was just a mere footnote in Western history books. They had been written out of history.

The silence was heavy and suffocating. It was occasionally disrupted by the loud cries and screams of my mother's sister, Aunty Hadia, who had arrived from Senegal where she lived with her husband and children. How could such a strong and thunderous voice come out of such a tiny body? I cried too, but I cried in silence, making sure to have a wrap on my face to catch all my tears. I cried until my pillow was soaked to the point where I had to toss it and find another one. Things slowly returned to normal in the household. My brother and I restarted school after a week at home. The women who had temporarily stopped coming for water in the morning resumed their ritual; Bailao loudly conversed with the neighbor's maid as they went about their daily activities, occasionally sharing a laugh. Things seemed to pick up where they had left off, except that my mother was no longer there to wake me up in the morning and help me get ready for school. No one asked me what I wanted to eat for lunch before I joyfully strolled to school. Bailao helped me put Karité oil in my braids, but she did not do it like Neneh did. I could no longer gaze into Neneh's big pretty eyes, the ones I had borrowed from her, as she often teasingly said to me.

Sometimes, as I drifted to sleep on the porch, I would suddenly come out of my slumber because I heard my mother's voice calling for me, only to sadly realize that she was not there. I rarely saw my father anymore, and I once heard the neighbor whispering to my aunt that he was spending all his time at a bar in Cosa. I wondered what a bar was, but from the tone in the neighbor's voice, I could tell that it wasn't a very holy place. For several weeks, we carried on with our new life. Aunty Hadia returned to Dakar after a couple of weeks. She had eventually stopped wailing; I couldn't be sure if it was because I had asked her about what my brother told me regarding crying for people who have passed, or just because she could no longer produce tears. I was glad she left as I could no longer take her boisterous ways; besides, I did not get on well with her youngest child. Bailao was spending more time with her friends and less time taking care of the house. I went to school a few days with crumpled uniforms because she had forgotten to iron them, and I was sent to Mr. Keita's office. Baba was still staying out a lot, sometimes not coming straight home after leaving work. Maybe he was at the bar? What was he doing there, I often wondered, and I sat on the front terrace watching the road, hoping to see his car point its nose at the top of the street toward the house. The street that led from the main road to our row of villas was lined with flamboyant trees that almost formed a tunnel. They looked majestic, and when they were in bloom, they were a feast for the eyes. Whenever the blooms eventually fell to the ground, they created a red carpet of flowers. I sometimes picked up a few and tucked them between the pages of my books. On occasion, I would try to count the trees while waiting for Baba's car to appear, but more often than not I lost count as the parallel trunks disappeared into each other in the distance and I had to start over.

On this day, Baba was home. It must have been a Sunday. My Uncle Abdul and his wife, Hassanatou, had arrived about a half hour before, and the three adults were deep in discussion in the living room. I was sitting at the dining room table, feigning interest in the book I had in front of me while listening in to the exchange. They had come for us. My uncle and his wife had come for my brothers and me. My uncle was facing my father, and his wife was sitting by his side. She took a sip of the cool water I had brought them and then gently rubbed her belly, which seemed even bigger while she was sitting down. I wondered when she was going to have her baby. She had been very close to my mother since she married my uncle. We sometimes visited her at their house in Kissosso. I often stared at her, but not too conspicuously. She was very pretty, and she almost looked like the models I sometimes saw in *Amina* magazine. She had fine facial features with a delicate, petite nose, her skin looked silky, and her hair was black and lustrous, which she had tied at the back of her head. My uncle had been doing most of the talking, while my father shook his head, occasionally stopping to turn in my direction and look at me. He finally spoke, and his voice was low, almost inaudible.

"So, you have come for my children? My children?" His voice got a little stronger on that last note.

"Only with your permission, Keynan," said my uncle, addressing him by the title one calls his or her older sister's husband. His wife went on to add, "Before leaving for Kamsar, Halimatou asked me to do only two things for her in the event that she did not make it back. She wanted me to help you look after your three children, and she wanted me to ensure that they all stay in school, especially Amina."

There was a silence for a moment before my uncle spoke again to his wife.

"Hassanatou, in her state she cannot go back and forth between Kissosso and Simbaya every day. It would not only be straining for her but also costly. We have a four-bedroom house and a lot of space around for the children. I can drop them off to school in the mornings on my way to work downtown, and we also…"

"Don't you think I can take care of my own children?" Baba interrupted.

"That is not what we meant, Keynan, we are just trying…"

"Trying to what? Help? I do not need help raising my own children, and you do not have to worry about them going to school. We have done fine so far, and we will manage." And with that he stood up, signaling that the conversation was over. My uncle stood up as well and helped his wife to her feet as he spoke again.

"Keynan, we know they are your children, and no one is trying to take them away from you; this is just a temporary solution. In the event that you marry again, we will return them to you. Just promise that you will think about it."

My father stopped for a second. It seemed as if he were getting ready to say something, but then he just moved toward the terrace and called for Bailao. "In the event you marry again..." that sentence fragment kept resonating in my ears. Was Baba getting a new wife? I looked up when he came back into the room, motioned for me to clear the dining table, and said as he turned to my uncle and his wife, "You should have something to eat before you leave. Come on, have a seat."

It would have been absolutely disgraceful to let our guests leave our house without offering them a meal, even if they had only been under our roof for a mere minute. This was a custom that couldn't be debased. When families did not have any food to offer their guests, they offered fresh water to appease their thirst. When I was home, it was my mission to bring fresh water to our guests as soon as they got seated. Usually Bailao would get busy setting up the table, but on that day, she was nowhere to be found, so I proceeded to the kitchen to get started on the task when Baba prompted me to.

After they left, I joined Baba on the porch. We sat quietly and watched my baby brother play with N'na Toman, the neighbor's daughter, who was four years old as well. Interestingly enough, our neighbors Mr. and Mrs. Fofana also had three children who were approximately the same age as us. We each had our pal. Idrissa had Karim who was almost sixteen, I had Mousto who was nine, and Ousbi had N'na Toman. We never knew her real name. She was called N'na Toman because Mr. Fofana had named her after his mother, and it would have been disrespectful to directly call her by her first name, so her nickname became N'na Toman—mother's namesake.

"Baba, are you getting a new wife?" I suddenly blurted out. He looked at me intently, picked me up, and sat me on his lap. He took a pause and smiled at me.

"Of course not, ma chérie," he finally answered. He did not add anything after that, and I did not make any further inquiries although I was anxious to do so. We were still quietly sitting on the porch when the muezzin's voice broke the silence, signaling that it was time for the dusk prayer.

Aunty Hassanatou came back the next day. She was in the kitchen when I came home for lunch, helping Ousbi feed himself. She came back every single day after that, and we were all getting used to seeing her around, usually sitting on a mat on the terrace, her legs spread out in front of her and her belly hanging, round and heavy. She gave orders, supervised, and ensured that Bailao was doing her daily tasks. My uncle picked her up on his way home from work in the evenings, and they drove off in their white Renault IV. Renault and Peugeot were the most popular cars in the city. My father drove a Renault IX, and most taxicabs in the city were Renault vehicles as well—rusty, yellow, worn-down vehicles that traveled the streets making clunking noises. There were also the magbanas, small vans that were converted to remove and replace the car seats with benches to fit more people inside. It wasn't unusual to see them speeding down the road with a bundle of luggage tied on to the car roof with passengers packed in like sardines, because drivers would squeeze a horde of twenty passengers in a vehicle that was meant for only ten people to maximize their profits. The magbanas also had a sinister aura about them. They were known as the "taxi de la mort," the death taxi, because when those overpacked cars got into accidents, no one survived.

Aunty Hassanatou kept coming back until one day, Bailao, after receiving her monthly remuneration, packed her bags and left without explanation. I felt abandoned because she did not say goodbye to me. I came back home to an empty room and wardrobe. She had been part of my life for as far as I could remember, and for the second time in a span of a few weeks, I felt complete helplessness and incomprehension. Neneh was gone. Now Bailao was, too. Everything became irreversibly different from that point. Bailao had been the bridge between my old life when Neneh had still been around and the new life we had. We shared a special bond that I was not sure I could replicate with Baba or my brothers. She told me folktales every night before I went to sleep. She sometimes told me scary stories, and on those nights, she had to tell me a funny story as well to make me forget about the frightening one. She had stories about princesses and mean witches and stories about the rabbit and the hyena. Those were my favorites, as the hyena relentlessly tried to trick the rabbit in all situations and the rabbit always managed to outsmart the hyena. She sang for me, lulling me to sleep with her soothing voice. Now she was gone. Since Bailao was no longer there to cook and clean, my father became more amenable to discussing our move to live with Aunty Hassanatou and Uncle Abdul. I could almost feel his misery the day they came for Ousbi and I. He had decided that Idrissa would stay with him since he was old enough, and we would visit on the weekends. I had not seen Baba cry since my mother died, and it broke my heart to watch him through the rear window of the car as we drove away.

Chapter Three

The temporary solution turned into a permanent one. My father died two years later. He never remarried. My mind was clouded with questions that a typical eleven-year-old would not likely entertain, and those questions still dash through my head on occasion. Baba had started drinking heavily after we left. He sometimes slept all day when we visited on the weekends. My brother Idrissa and I usually escaped to the rooftop on those days while Ousbi went to play with N'na Toman. It was our retreat. We were on top of everything, and we shared our secrets. I often remembered how Neneh would get upset because

I climbed the tree that led to the roof or because I spent some days running around the neighborhood with my brother and his friends. "Little girls do not climb trees, and they certainly do not run around dragging wooden trucks with a bunch of boys." I could almost hear her voice. I was sometimes puzzled by her comments, because no sooner had she finished explaining acceptable conduct for a well-behaved little girl, she would go on to tell me that whatever a boy can do, I also could, and that I should not let anyone convince me otherwise. I was often uncertain of how to interpret her remarks.

While sitting on the roof, we sometimes inched closer to the edge so that we could observe what was happening around the neighborhood as we told each other about our lives. He told me that Baba had been coming home very late on most days and that he slept a lot. My brother sometimes had to go to the bar in Cosa and convince him to come home. Baba gave him money for food every morning, and he had been saving a portion of it; just in case, he answered when I asked him why. He had turned seventeen and was about to graduate high school. He sometimes showed me picture cutouts from magazines, raving about the newest Adidas shoes or shiny sports cars. Other times we talked about Poupette, the girl he had a crush on, and his plan to sneak the car out of the driveway. I eagerly looked forward to those moments so that I could come out of the shell that I had started enveloping myself in.

Our new place was nothing like our home in Simbaya. It was a big white house sitting at the bottom of a hill. On a clear day, you could see the peak of Mount Kakoulima in the distance. We barely had any neighbors as the very few houses in the neighborhood were loosely scattered. Electricity was almost nonexistent, and once night fell, the house was pitch dark and had to be illuminated with storm lanterns and candles. The lanterns occasionally released a puff of black smoke, and the kerosene that fueled it had an unpleasant smell. On our first evening there, I was perplexed by the woman walking around the neighborhood at dusk, screaming at the top of her lungs "Karassin!! Sassery!!" I found out when she was hailed by my uncle that she sold kerosene and mosquito repellents. *Karassin* was a variation of the word *kerosene* in the local dialect, and *sassery* literally meant mosquito medicine in the Soso dialect. She used a small can that once contained tomato paste to measure the kerosene, and she sold it by the cup. At bedtime, Aunty Hassanatou lit the mosquito repellents and placed them in strategic locations around the house. The smoke that it released had a unique, overpowering smell, and one could plainly see the mosquitoes falling to the ground if they paid close attention. In addition to the repellents, all the beds in the house had a mosquito net. Once set around the bed, it made it look like a little cocoon. Sliding into the bed and under the net at night gave me a certain sense of security, as if nothing could touch me.

The darkness that surrounded the house at night was frightening. The only sound that could be heard was that of the frogs croaking in the nearby pond like a symphony. I felt lost in the unfamiliar setting, and I knew that my little brother, Ousbi, did as well. There were only a handful of children in the locality, none of which went to school or were our age. Our house was a very short distance from a swamp mangrove where I sometimes went to get lost. I would sit on top of one of the rocks and daydream about my life in Simbaya. I would imagine that it had all been a very bad dream, and I would picture my whole family sitting in the calmness of our terrace on a lazy afternoon, enjoying a meal and sharing laughter, just like it used to be. I frequently lost track of time and was only brought back to reality by the movement of the crabs in the swampy mangrove mud as the tide started rising again in the late afternoon.

Was it a simple but cruel coincidence that my father died in the same hospital as Neneh had? Idrissa had been the caretaker this time. He took a bus to the hospital and often missed school because of the lengthy trip. He brought Baba meals because the food they gave him at the hospital made him feel even sicker. Koto—big brother, as I called him—changed during that time. I could sense that something had hardened inside him. He laughed less often and looked worried every time he came to see us in Kissosso. He left in the evening with bowls of food tied in a plastic bag, his shoulders slumped, and trekked up the hill to catch a magbana. My uncle had asked him to come live with us, but he refused, preferring to stay by himself. After Baba's death, he had to vacate the property, so he moved out of the villa and went to live with his friend Maurice. Our lives had been torn asunder by the loss of our parents, and we now had to survive any way we could.

Somewhere between the time my father died and the subsequent years, I reached the conclusion that I was being punished by God for something that was utterly unknown to me. How else could anyone explain the fact that the dearest people in my life had been taken away from me? First it was Neneh, then Bailao, then Baba. Was I also going to lose my brothers? Then what? Would I be next in line? I was very quiet all the time, but I was hopping mad on the inside, and most of the time I was just achingly sad. The well-meaning attempts from a few family members to give me comforting answers only made me sink a little deeper. "Everything happens for a reason sweetheart.... God must have his reasons for taking them back." I would sometimes retort, "What is the reason?" That question was more than often met with blank stares or another vague answer like "May the earth rest lightly on them; at least they are in Heaven now." I eventually stopped voicing my questions, retreating instead into the safe shield of my bubble, but they still followed me like a gloomy shadow over my head.

Getting accustomed to our new lifestyle was one of the hardest things I ever had to do, but it was also one of the blessings I will always be thankful for as it was this changing period that prepared me for the many other adjustments I would have to become quickly skilled at as I transitioned through life. The manner in which Aunty Hassanatou, whom I also called Aunty, ran her household was somewhat analogous to a small training camp. The women of the house, meaning my aunt; Batouly, the girl who had been sent from the village to help my aunt with household tasks after she gave birth to her first baby; and myself were always the first to rise at the crack of dawn. Having to complete domestic chores came as a shock to me as I had never had to do this before, and I smugly assumed that it would be Batouly's responsibility. My morning duties started with sweeping the courtyard with a handmade broom, which was an assemblage of stiff grasses tied at the top by a string. The broom did not have a handle, so the task had to be completed while bending down. On school days, once finished with my sweeping task, I would start a fire on the charcoal stove to boil the breakfast kinkeliba tea before proceeding to get ready for school. Batouly would then take over to warm up some water for the baby's bath in a large aluminum pot. The rest of us took cold showers in the morning, and if there was the slightest hint of sleepiness left in you, that shower certainly did an outstanding job of invigorating you. My uncle usually brought bread home each evening on his way from work, but on the mornings when we ran out, we purchased more from the bread lady who went door to door each morning, balancing a large platter of bread on her head while carrying her baby on her back. I always wondered how she so skillfully did this without seemingly putting any effort into it. She was always on time, arriving at our front step whether we needed bread or not. On the rare occasions when she was late, my little brother, Ousbi, was sent to the small convenience store on top of the hill to pick up the bread.

The morning chores were seamlessly completed every day under the watch of Aunty Hassanatou. Similarly, the evening tasks where precisely coordinated and completed. My evening duties consisted of refilling the lamps with kerosene, cleaning the grime left by the black smoke on the bulb glass that protected the flame, and placing the lighted lamps around the house. Batouly and Aunty usually prepared dinner in the outdoor kitchen while I did my homework under the dining room's glowing lamp. Every now and then, I looked intently at the flame, thinking back on my last conversation with my mother. "You are a lamp in the darkness." I tried to understand the meaning of the words, but I generally concluded my thoughts with the fact that I did not feel like I was a lamp; and if I were in fact a lamp, then my flame surely wasn't glistening.

My old tendency of sleeping in on the weekends was also broken up as I had to rise at daybreak and carry on with my tasks. In addition to my daily assignments, during the weekend, I was in charge of washing and ironing all our school uniforms and my uncle's shirts. We did not have a washing machine like the one in Simbaya that Bailao struggled to use every time, where she had to call me in the middle of a cartoon to help her start it. I was in awe that you could put dirty laundry in a machine and, a half hour later, pull it out sparkling clean. Since we didn't have the magic machine, I did the laundry by hand using a washing board and three large basins—one for the soapy water, the second for the first rinse, and the last for the final rinse. I was shaky and awkward at first with the washing board but soon enough got the hang of it. When I was done, my hands were usually wrinkly, and my little brother often made fun of my granny hands. The laundry dried all day on clotheslines, and in the rainy season, it sometimes took several days to dry due to the capricious weather.

The highlight of my weekend was the Sunday trip to the market. Aunty Hassanatou entrusted me with an amount of money that seemed considerably large in my eyes and sent me off to the market to pick the condiments for that day's meals. In the beginning, she took me with her on Saturdays, and I observed as she dealt and bargained with the various vendors while working her way seamlessly across the crowded market. The first day I was sent alone, I was terrified and convinced that I would not remember to get all the condiments or that the vendors would laugh at this little girl trying to bargain with them. I was even more petrified at the idea that I would lose the money I had been entrusted with. The apprehension was lifted once I got to the market, and I realized that most of the vendors recognized me and actually helped me pick out the best produce, promising me the best prices if I came back to them the next time around. Merchants competed for my attention, waving goods in front of me or calling out, "Hello there, pretty girl, come see my stand; I have the freshest okra in this whole market," while breaking the tip of the vegetable to prove their point; another stirred through her pail of palm oil and scooped it up to show me its fluidity and rich, red color. I loved going to the market because it was vibrant and buoyant, with a triumph of colorful vegetable displays that seemed to go on forever. I always made a stop in the fabrics section although I had absolutely no dealings to complete there. I just loved looking at the assortments of opulent and multicolored textiles and basking in their cheerfulness. I felt alive and happy in the booming commotion of the marketplace, and at times, for very brief moments, I felt in control of my emotions and destiny.

The other highlight of my week was going to school. I was always excited to hop in the white Renault IV with Ousbi and Uncle and drive off to school. I enthusiastically looked forward to school because it was the only part of my life that had remained almost unchanged, so it became my new haven. I saw the same friendly faces every day and went about the same activities. I say it was almost unchanged, because one thing had changed. My little brother and I had become the kids who did not go home at lunchtime since our new house was too far from the school. We would have to take the bus, then walk another twenty minutes before arriving home. I was given an allowance each morning for the both of us, but we rarely bought any food around the school. We continued our lunch rotations among my friends' houses, and I used part of the allowance money to buy snacks for the whole group and hid part of it in my armoire at home. When I accumulated enough money, I took the bus to the airport with one my friends, Fatima, and spent hours browsing through the airport magazine concession stand, flipping through the latest *OK!* magazine, *Femme Actuelle*, *Paris Match*, or *Amina* magazine before finally buying one for myself and another for Fatima. I often thought about the lives of the people in the magazines; they always looked so picture perfect and happy. I imagined myself living their life, wearing fancy clothes, jet-setting around the world, and meeting interesting people without a worry in my life.

Chapter Four

The fragile routine of my new life was interrupted by the sudden emergence of one archaic practice that I just couldn't fathom. On one clammy evening, my mother's sister, Aunty Hawa, came for me as it was time to perform the traditional female excision that each girl had to go through before their first period. I had just turned twelve, and the timing was auspicious. The ghastly custom required the removal of the clitoris from the female genitalia in order to suppress sexual desire and pleasure. I had read in my magazines that the tradition was not only prevalent in many parts of Africa but also in some parts of Asia. It had been around for centuries and was carried out in many cultures in an attempt to "tame" young girls before they reached their teenage years, to make them respectable and clean young women; however, the barbaric ritual that was medically unproven and unnecessary was unspeakably inhumane and it was just another way to demean women. Aunty Hassanatou asked me to gather a few of my clothes as I would be staying at Aunty Hawa's house for a short period. We were on school break, so it clearly had been carefully planned. I knew the day would come, but I was utterly surprised by the lack of preamble, the casualness in which Aunty Hawa told me about it as if she were asking me to go pick up some bread from the kitchen while Aunty Hassanatou picked the bones out of the smoked fish for her soup— there was an entire absence of decorum in the whole thing. After all, they were planning on taking a piece of me, cutting it from my body just like one would saw a limb off a tree and discard it, never to be found again.

"You are not going to need that," Batouly sneered as I picked up a dress from the armoire. I looked back at her sharply. "So you knew!"

"Of course, they have been discussing it for some time now."

"And it never occurred to you to tell me!" I snapped back.

"Don't bite my head off! What did you expect to happen?

Telling you wouldn't change a thing," she sneered again. I did not have the energy for an argument, so I finished packing my things, silent and apprehensive.

My genital mutilation was executed in the back of a house that seemed abandoned. Aunty Hawa woke me up at five in the morning, and we set out on a long walk to the midwife's quarters in the dark. I was sleepy and kept tripping on the rocks covering the road, both from nervousness and not being able to see the road clearly. Once we arrived, the midwife, who was a chubby woman with a black headscarf tied around her head, whispered a few words to my aunt before leading me out of the house unceremoniously to a building that looked like it was crumbling. The woman knelt in front of me and spread my legs. There, in half darkness, on a rustic mat, with a rural knife, the procedure was done while pain shot through my whole body and tears trickled down my cheeks while Aunty Hawa firmly pinned my legs to the floor.

The acute pain and discomfort I experienced then and in the following weeks was something that I loathed thinking about even afterward. Aunty Hawa, who was also a midwife, gave me sitz baths every morning followed by first aid care, which was a thing that most girls who underwent this procedure never got and who sometimes ended up battling life-threatening infections. The period between my excision and my initiation ceremony was supposed to be a character-building phase for me.

Everything I did during that period, according to the belief, would determine my character for the remainder of my life, so it was of utmost importance that I act like a reverent young lady, show tolerance for pain that would be a constant part of my life as a woman, and be able to accomplish all domestic duties that would be expected of a young bride. I wore the same ritualistic white percale wrap every day for six weeks, removing it only to be washed, and I sat on the bed with a towel wrapped around me as I waited for my sole outfit to dry. I understood what Batouly had meant. As I tried to comprehend why I had to go through this ordeal, I often wondered if my mother would have carried on this tradition with me. I was unsure of the answer, but nevertheless, I convinced myself that my mother would not have subjected me to such torment, and I silently swore to myself that I would never in my lifetime inflict this horrid practice on anyone.

My initiation ceremony, which symbolically marked my transition from girlhood to womanhood, was a celebration of the fact that I had successfully completed the ritual process. I was covered with gifts and praise while women sang and danced around me. As the commotion went on, I speculated on the meaning of womanhood and what it entailed, because even after everything was done, I still felt like the twelve-year-old I was.

My relationship with Aunty Hassanatou had become shaky over the past few years. Her unwavering outlook on life was starkly different from my mother's. Her compassion never translated into affection, except for her own two children. We never hugged, and I never dreamed of even the slightest hope of receiving a goodnight kiss. We did not converse like I had with my mother, and on the rare occasions when I spoke to her, I stayed a few feet of distance away; in fact, I rarely came close to her because I had grown frightened of her vacillating moods—cheery one minute then irate and irascible the next because I accidentally broke the lantern's glass while cleaning it or I did not speak loudly enough. She would sometimes immediately soften her tone after becoming conscious of her own behavior.

"Don't mind her, oh; she is a constant pregnant woman," Batouly would say when I asked her how she stayed so stoic when she was on the other end of the revilements. At this time, Aunty Hassanatou was expecting her third child and had been irritable. Whether her mood swings were caused by her consecutive pregnancies or some other factor, the damage was already done. I sought out reasons not to come home right after school, enrolling into extracurricular activities and convincing my uncle to get me a permanent-member card to the French cultural center. My more indulgent uncle often got into arguments with Aunty Hassanatou because of his leniency and allowing me to almost always do as I pleased. Time and again, I yearned to be closer to her, but my efforts were usually met with what I thought at the time was cool indifference. As I grew up, I started understanding the trials and tribulations of the common African woman— the qualms she faced every day in raising not only her own children but also carrying on the responsibility of successfully bringing me up uncorrupted, educated, and also domestically fit, along with my little brother; her running of a full household on a meager salary while my uncle was away at work most of the time; and most important, my comprehension of the fact that giving affection wasn't the pinnacle of her priorities in those times. I started grasping the idea that it wasn't in fact a lack of concern on her part; instead, we just shared similar, but also at the same time entirely different, realities.

The dated traditions in our culture relegated women to the back with no voice of their own. My aunt was different as she undeniably made her voice heard whenever possible. She was very much like my mother in that manner. However, there was always a perimeter and an extent to which she would voice her view, because at the end of the day, the only opinion that mattered was that of her husband—or father had she been unmarried. Once wedded, a woman was at the service of her spouse and his family, abandoning her say, personality, distinction, and desires to merge with those of the new man in her life. Her worth was consequently measured by the number of children she mothered. Aunty had been attending a vocational school to become a secretary when she got married and was uprooted from her native Mamou to the big city. She had been a housewife since. My uncle's duty as man of the house, as well as the typical man in our culture, was completed once he put money on the table for expenses. Whether it was enough or not, it became the woman's responsibility to figure out how to properly allocate it among food, household needs, clothing, children's needs, and miscellaneous and unexpected expenditures. When my aunt sometimes protested that there was not enough money to cover the day's expenses, my uncle just shrugged off and retorted, "Figure it out."

One morning, after a heated argument, my uncle left without leaving any money and without waiting for Ousbi and I to get in the car to be dropped off at school. My aunt stormed into her bedroom, teary eyed, as I stood still in the living room unsure of what to do. She shortly reemerged with a new spring in her step. She pulled me aside and gestured for Ousbi to go finish his breakfast. Her voice was grave when she spoke, looking at me straight in the eye. "This is why you are going to school, so that you won't depend on someone to dictate your future to you. Whenever in doubt, remember that." She paused for a second before adding, "You and Ousbi wait here; I will take you to school." She promptly changed, and we walked to the embarkation stop to hail a taxi, with Ousbi and I walking a few steps behind her. Once she dropped us off to school, she did not get out of the taxi; instead, she directed the driver to take her downtown.

When she came back later that evening, she had officially enrolled in training school to become a teller at a bank. There were more arguments that night, my uncle and aunt's voices echoing from their bedroom while I lay still on the bed staring at the ceiling. They did not talk to each other the next morning. The ambience in the house was uncomfortable for a few days, but Aunty did not relent, and a month later, she too started getting in the car with us in the morning to be dropped off at school.

Chapter Five

Every time it rained, I would think about my mother, and it every so often brought a smile to my face. It was the tradition for the neighborhood children to run outside at the first drop of rain. It seemed so exhilarating and free. When I asked my mother why I couldn't play in the rain, she humorously replied, "Because you are my little sugar, and you would melt in the rain."

The slamming of the door brought me out of my reverie. Batouly was rushing to grab covers out of the armoire. Every time it started thundering, she hastily moved around covering all the mirrors in the house. It was a common belief among many people that leaving mirrors exposed during a storm attracted lightning. The look of panic on her face as she hurried around always made me grin. I peeked out of the window, and Mount Kakoulima in the distance was almost invisible under the angry, dark clouds. I was in the bedroom we shared, reading the latest novel I had gotten my hands on. Since we started high school, Fatima, Mamady, Oumi, and I had moved on from rotating lunchtimes at each other's houses to swapping books. We scouted the French cultural center and library for the latest titles. When there were none left, we searched the markets for book peddlers. They were rare, but we could sometimes find them in corners of the market with piles of books thrown on a piece of cloth spread out on the ground. The pile usually had an indiscriminate mixture of books in Russian, French, English, and occasionally characters that we assumed to be Chinese. There were books on astronomy, communism, quantum physics, history, and other random subjects. On our lucky days, we scored French literature classics—Molière, Victor Hugo, Honoré de Balzac, Guy de Maupassant. We sometimes argued over who got what or who would get the first turn before coming to a consensus. If all else failed, a coin toss was always a viable option in the decision-making process.

After school, I always hurried home to finish my household chores, then buried myself in the bedroom, losing myself in books. Léopold Sédar Senghor, Aimé Césaire, Djibril Tamsir Niane, Mariame Bâ, Camara Laye, Williams Sassine. They were all my new best friends. Their words in all their splendor brought me inspiration and hope. They spoke to the fraught soul within me. They told stories, spoke of Négritude, acquainted me with early African Francophone literature, and engrossed me in glorious poems—and I devotedly immersed myself in them. That was also the time I discovered Bob Marley. I grew up hearing his music in market stands or wherever there was a gathering of young men making Ataya tea, but I had no idea who he was and what he represented to reggae music and the Rastafarian movement. The enlightenment came from my cousin Aziz, who had come from Paris to complete a year of high school in his native country and learn about his culture. He was obsessed with Bob Marley, and I, too, soon became passionate about the story, the man, and the music.

My dream to attend Sainte Marie went up in flames as the tuition was simply unaffordable for my new family. Koto also had to drop out of the school and enroll in the local public high school the year my father died. The disappointment of not attending Sainte Marie was eventually softened by the fact that I still had my friends. Throughout high school, we had all started growing into our respective personalities and some of our paths diverged. Fatima and I had turned seventeen, and we spent more time together. Mamady, along with the other boys in our class, had suddenly developed a heightened interest in girls and spent most of his time drooling over magazines pictures behind the stairwells and writing love letters copied from poetry books. Oumi spent less time with us, too, because she was the only one who had decided to specialize in experimental science as her orientation in high school, while the rest of us had decided to focus on social studies. Before entering high school, we had to choose between three options available for incoming freshmen. We all studied the same disciplines, except that the mathematical sciences option emphasized math and physics, the experimental sciences option put emphasis on biology and chemistry, and the social studies option stressed history, languages, literature, and civic studies. Oumi wanted to be a doctor; Fatima, a professor; I wanted to become a journalist; and Mamady had no idea, so he just trailed us most of the time.

As the baccalauréat loomed around, I started spending countless hours studying for the exam, because failing it was not an option. I knew deep down that I would pass it, but I often got little panic attacks imagining what would happen if I didn't. "An education is your ticket to a brighter future." Those words resonated in my ears. They had come from my chemistry teacher Ms. Tawel, a tall, fierce, dark woman with an afro and a staunch supporter of girls' right to an education. I heard that after school, she circulated the markets looking for school-aged girls who were attending to merchandise stalls and visited families to convince them that their girls, too, could go to school and succeed at it. She was the only female teacher at the school, and I admired her. I often watched her as she laughed freely, propped on a classroom table with her feet on the bench while eating her lunch and rebuking something one of the other teachers had said. She reminded me of my mother. Was it the afro? Or the khaki pants she wore religiously every day? Or maybe the way she always spoke with conviction? Whatever it was, something about her brought my mother to mind, and I hung on to every word she said. "An education is your ticket to a brighter future. Remember it!" She often said this at the end of class, directly addressing the girls in the room. I sometimes wished I could spend more time with her outside of school. I wished I could carry her brown leather satchel for her as she walked home just so I could listen to her talk.

Even with the baccalauréat in my pocket, I would still have to pass an additional competitive exam to gain a seat at the University of Conakry because places were limited. The students who couldn't go abroad to study wanted to at least be in the capital city. Failing to obtain a place on the Conakry campus meant that I would have to go to a smaller school in the country since I could not afford to attend a private university. Koto had gotten a state scholarship to study in Morocco after he passed the baccalauréat at the top of his class. His friend Maurice's father had pulled some strings at the education ministry to help. I cried for days when he left, wondering when, or if, I would ever see him again. "You are being dramatic," he said when he hugged me tight in the airport departure hall the day he left, but I saw it—I saw the sadness in his eyes as he spoke. He often sent me pictures of Rabat; his room so that I could see where he slept; foods I had never seen before; and one of him with Maurice, their hands resting on each other's shoulders, both smiling wildly with the ocean in the background. I cherished those photos and tucked them in a notebook that I hid in the back of my armoire.

Some students at my high school had already started planning for their first year of college in Morocco, France, London, or some other faraway place. I daydreamed of going to a prestigious university, maybe la Sorbonne in Paris. Senghor had attended la Sorbonne, even if only briefly, and so had Cheikh Anta Diop. What would it be like to sit in the amphitheaters where they, too, had once sat as freshmen? To walk the halls they had walked? But I quickly shut down those thoughts. What was the use, anyway? So, I went back to my books.

Fatima's parents were preparing a visa for her to travel to Canada right after our exam. They hoped she would pass the exam and get admitted to a Canadian school while she was there. We spent hours talking about it, imagining what her life would be like. We had even started picking through her belongings, sorting between what she would take and what she would leave behind; we even went to the Madina market to pick out the outfit she would wear to travel. I was thrilled and happy for her, even though I sometimes felt a twinge of envy in the midst of all the excitement. But mostly, I felt sad— sad that we would soon be separated. We had grown up together and had been tied at the hip for most of my life, and I did not know how I would handle this new change. Whenever I became a bit quiet, Fatima sometimes noticed and tried to comfort me. "You know, once I am in Montreal and enrolled at uni, I will find a job and an apartment, and we will get you enrolled maybe for next year. Don't worry, we will be reunited before you know it. I will not stop until you are in Canada with me, my *Bobo*." We would laugh and hug each other, both of us only half believing that.

"Do you see that?"

I was studying for my exams on a hot afternoon, sitting on the terrace with Batouly, when she caught my attention.

"What am I supposed to see?"

"The car," Batouly said as she pointed toward the hill. Slowly inching its way down the road was a red car, going almost in a zigzag pattern in its effort to avoid the protruding rocks from the road.

"Hmm...that's odd. They must be lost." Uncle Abdul's white Renault was the only car we were accustomed to seeing coming down the hill when he and Aunty Hassanatou were returning from the city in the evening, signaling us to tidy up the living room, turn off the TV, scatter the few neighborhood kids toward the backyard, and roll the TV stand back to the master bedroom. We had power every other day now, and ever since Uncle came home one day with a TV and had a parabolic antenna installed, the house had turned into the meeting point for the neighborhood youth, where everyone sat on the tiled floor and stared in awe at the images dancing on the screen. It was mostly French variety shows as all the channels were French—TF1, France 2, France 3, France 4. When the national programs started, it was mostly the news in the different dialects, followed by Brazilian soap operas that we understood nothing about, but our eyes remained glued to the screen, not wanting to miss a second of it. Mr. Bangoura, the other car owner of the neighborhood, lived right at the top of the hill, and I could see his blue Peugeot parked in the courtyard like a centerpiece while the household busied itself around it, going about its daily activities. The car, a red Nissan, had now crossed the last intersection and was headed straight to our house.

Batouly and I stood up from our wooden stools when the car turned into the gravel driveway. I tried to make out who it was as the car stopped.

"Assalam wallaykum!" said an older man as he got out from the passenger side. "Is Abdul home?" The familiarity in which he had greeted us and asked about my uncle hinted that he knew him.

"On djaramaa. He is not in at the moment, but he should be arriving anytime now. Please have a seat." I made my way toward the terrace to pull out a chair.

"Hello." A young man emerged from the back seat of the car. I had not noticed him at first. He stepped forward and held his hand out.

"Hello," I said as I grabbed his hand to quickly shake it. He smiled, and I hurriedly walked up the steps and directed the men to the seats on the terrace. The driver got out of the car and found a seat under the shade of the mango tree outside. I glanced to where Batouly had been standing, but she was no longer there. I turned to go to the kitchen when the old man spoke.

"You must be Halimatou's daughter...Aminatou, right?" I stopped and turned back toward him.

"Yes. I go by Amina."

"You look just like your mother, MashAllah."

I looked down and walked away, wondering who the man was. He had known my mother. He was maybe a relative, but I certainly had never seen him before. I went to the kitchen and found Batouly preparing a couple of glasses and fresh water in a pitcher to serve to the guests.

"I have never seen them before, have you?" I asked. She shook her head.

"I wonder why they are here..." I whispered. She shrugged and headed to the terrace. Batouly was not talkative. I often wondered about her life in the village where she had come from—what was it like? Who had she

53

left behind? Had she been coerced into taking this job in the city or did she have a say? Did she miss her home? But whenever I asked questions, she gave short, vague answers and busied herself with her tasks, sometimes humming a tune as she went through the motions of grinding, sifting, stirring...so I did not press her. I went back to the living room and peeked through the window to have a good look at the guests. The old man wore a white caftan with some white babouches and a white prayer hat. The standard uniform, one could say. If he were to come out of a mosque now, I would not have been able to pick him out of the crowd of the other old men who would also be wearing white caftans with white hats and babouches. He took a sip of his water, while with his right hand, his fingers moved along his white-and-gold prayer beads in a continuous movement, one bead after the other. The young man, on the other hand, stood out. He does not live here, I thought to myself. I could tell from his complexion. He had that matte complexion of people who had just arrived from Europe and had not yet been burned by the ardent African sun, just like our neighbor Mrs. Touré's sister, when she had visited the prior summer. Baghifadé, that is the name they are given. Just arrived. Fresh off the plane. But that was not all. His clothes were extremely clean, his shirt a crisp, blinding white that you only saw in commercials. The white that had not yet been tainted by the reddish dust of Conakry, which turned our white high school uniform shirt into a yellowish, off-white color. His nails were clean, even; and his sneakers almost as white as his shirt. Definitely baghifadé. I smiled. Why the red pants, though? I don't know why, but I always found it odd to see a man wearing red pants. He was not particularly handsome, but not ugly, either. His features were the kind that could easily blend and fade into a group of faces. I was not sure why they were here to see my uncle, but I was going to find out.

I decided to go to my room and read to kill some time before Uncle Abdul arrived. My chores were minimal now, and I no longer had to clean lamp bulbs every night—only on the nights when we did not have power. If only we could get an air-conditioning unit in our room like the one that had gotten installed in Uncle and Aunty's bedroom the week before, life would be good, I thought as I stretched out on the bed with my book. I must have drifted off to sleep because I was awoken much later by the sound of a car starting. I jumped off the bed and hurried to peek out of the window. The red Nissan was backing out of the driveway. "Oh no," I mumbled. I had been planning on sitting on the terrace steps and pretending to read when Uncle Abdul got home so that I could listen in on his conversation with the guests. Jut great! I thought, and there was no way I could get anything out of Batouly. It was almost dusk, so I walked out of the room but made a sharp stop in the hallway when I heard Uncle Abdul and Aunty Hassanatou talking.

"Well, Amina is still young," said my uncle.

"The same age as when you plucked me out of my parents' house."

I could not see him, but I could almost hear my uncle smiling. What were they talking about?

"Well, not one word to her for now; I have to reach out to her paternal uncles first." I felt a pang. It all dawned on me at once. The old man. The young man. That expression on his face when he had said that I looked just like my mother; the way that the young man had coyly looked at me at the mention of my name as if to convey, but also withhold, something. They had come for me. I had heard countless stories like this, starting with Aunty Hassanatou. Girl develops a chest, girl turns seventeen or eighteen, girl starts to have more womanly features, word gets around that girl is turning into a fine young woman, and girl finishes high school with a head full of dreams, only to have them shattered by someone else's dream of snatching girl away at her ripe age and turning her into a domestic, child-rearing body that cooks and cleans for everyone; girl will gradually fade into the background, assimilating her dreams into her husband's, attending weekend baby naming or wedding ceremonies for another young girl whose dreams were also snatched from her. I felt hot and sweaty all of a sudden, even though it was cool in the house. I spun around and sped back to the bedroom. I could not go out there right now; I needed to be alone to untangle the million thoughts that were swirling in my head.

I feigned sleep later that evening when Batouly came around calling me for dinner. I had no desire to eat. I was consumed with anxiety and fear of what was going to happen now. Would I go to university? Would I even get to take my exams? Who were they? Where had they come from? Why me? Why now? Had Uncle and Aunty known all along? Was this it for me? Tears rolled down my cheeks. In moments of uncertainty like this one, I always thought of my mother. It wasn't until I reached my teenage years that I shed true tears of sorrow over my mother's death, when the reality with all its heaviness hit me. Every time I thought about my mother, I felt a dull pain in my stomach. I couldn't make up my mind about what was more agonizing—the fact that I never really got to know her because our time together had been abruptly cut short; the fact that I would never again have that intimate relationship between mother and daughter, the kind where a whole conversation can take place with just an exchange of looks; or the thought that she had died alone in a hospital in Kamsar with no close family present to hold her hand. My father had been traveling to Kamsar every other day to see her when she was in the hospital, splitting his time between her and us, the children. It took half a day to drive there, and he would sometimes take Idrissa with him. The day she died, Baba was with us. As excruciating as it was, I often wondered what her final moments had been like. Was she alone? Did anyone hold her hand? Did anyone comfort her? What was she feeling? Did she yearn for her children and her husband? Was she scared? Sometimes, in my dreams, I saw myself coming to her rescue, swiftly moving her away from harm, and us sharing a big laugh about that fool, death. I always woke up from those dreams with tears of joy and laughter in my eyes. But now these were anxious tears. Why was this happening? I wiped the tears off. I had to see Fatima, I thought as I turned and tried to go to sleep, knowing all too well that I would not find sleep that night.

The following days were uneventful but mired with a cloud of dark thoughts. The men did not return, and life was as normal as it could be, except that I could not get that conversation between Uncle and Aunty out of my head. Fatima tried to console me when I ran to her early the next morning. She tried to convince me in her naivete that maybe I was overreacting and that maybe that was not why the men had come to the house. She was deluded, I thought to myself. Why else would they have come? That weekend, while everyone in the household was drowning in slothfulness after a particularly heavy lunch, Aunty Hassanatou called me to help her carry some bags to Mrs. Kaba's house. Aunty had started selling clothes on the side to supplement her salary from her bank teller job, and whenever she had new items, we made the rounds of the houses in the neighborhood. We walked up the hill to Mrs. Kaba's house, carrying two heavy bags of clothes. I felt weighed down not only by the load I was carrying in my hands but also by the one in my stomach—a plate full of tchiep with chunky pieces of meat followed by a big glass of ginjan and bissap, or as I called it, ginssap. I had discovered that mixing the spicy ginger juice with the tart hibiscus juice created a delicious concoction that titillated the taste buds. I was out of breath when we got to Mrs. Kaba's house. She called out from inside for us to come in when we reached the front door. She was sitting on the sofa, taking up almost half of the space.

"Hello, hello, please come in; have a seat!" she cheerfully said while she removed the bags next to her. I hurried and sat on the side chair, next to Aunty. I looked around me while they carried on with greetings and formalities. I usually did not go beyond the courtyard whenever I came over to either borrow or return something. The living room was overstuffed. China plates, Russian dolls, porcelain figurines, and various knickknacks competed for space in an oversized china cabinet. The wall was covered with photographs, and the living room chairs all had pieces of ornate white lace on its arms and headrests. It looked like a djinn's house, as Koto would say, and I wanted to leave already. I tried to tune them both out, but that was short lived.

"So, dear, I hear you may soon have your own household..."

My heart skipped a beat. I looked at Mrs. Kaba to make sure she was addressing me, and sure enough, she was beaming with one of those big, overdone smiles while looking straight at me.

"Wh...what...I don't know," I stuttered and intertwined my fingers, glancing in Aunty's direction. She looked on and did not say anything. This was not a sales visit. I wanted to get up and run as fast as I could out of there, but I could not move.

"Well, it is about that time now. How old are you? About eighteen? I think you and my Hadja are the same age."

"I will turn eighteen in two months."

"Ah yes, ma fille, you are a woman now indeed.... Mahawa!!" she yelled out suddenly, startling both Aunty and me. "Are the drinks going to serve themselves? Oh god, I tell you, this girl...I don't know what to do with her." The smell of the incense burning slowly in a clay pot in the corner of the room suddenly became overwhelming.

"I don't even know anything about him," I cried out.

"Well, you know, I got married at sixteen.... I met him on the day of wedding." She laughed exuberantly. "You young kids now, you are lucky, oh!" Her laugh turned into a cough.

Aunty finally spoke. "Amina has not met him yet, so I would like for you to help me talk to her about this major step. You know, being a mother of two beautiful young ladies who are already married, I figured you have a lot of wisdom to impart." The women had obviously had a prior conversation.

"Oh yes, yes...of course, dear. This is an important

milestone in your life, Amina. We women always get to this point eventually, when we have to say goodbye to our families and go into another." I looked at her moving lips and wondered how many other young girls were sitting through this same speech at that very moment.

"Everything in your life has been in preparation for this, ma fille." I wished she would stop calling me that.

"But I don't know him! I did not choose him," I repeated.

"Oh honey...God chooses for you, and he brought this young man into your life," Aunty said while picking up my hand and holding it between her two palms. "You know Aunty Kadiatou who lives in Belle-Vue, right? Well, this is her first son. You do not know him because he left for the US when you were very young to go and study. You know his sisters, Bijou and Bebe. He comes from a good family, he is young, and he does not have another wife. Besides, our families have known each other for years; refusing this proposal would put a serious strain on our relationship." Silence fell for a moment.

"He is a good man, he did very good studies, he is working, and now he wants a family," Mrs. Kaba chimed in. "I know your generation is all about love marriages, but sweetie, love will come after; just give him a chance. Look at me: I have been married for twenty-two years, and I am happy, probably more so than some couples in love marriages." Mrs. Kaba's gaze was fixed on something unknown. How would she even know about who this man was? I thought to myself.

"Do I have to, Aunty?" I asked, pleading.

"I have no say, Amina. Your uncle and I are just intermediaries in this thing; as you know, your paternal uncles are the ones with the final decision," she answered, still holding my hand.

"Will I still attend university?"

"If you get married before, it would be up to your spouse," she said, resigned.

"Can you make it a condition, please?" I pleaded with her, pressing her hands.

"You know very well that it is not up to me to impose anything; that depends on your uncles. But he seems like a sensible young man; I do not think he would ask you to give up your studies."

"Please, Aunty, I am begging you; can you please talk to them...please?"

"I will try, but do not make this a big drama. Many women have done this before you, and they are doing just fine. You will be fine too, Amina. At the very least, get to know him. He is coming over next Saturday, and the two of you would have a chance to speak and get to know each other," she added in a final way, indicating that nothing further would be added. She opened the bag of clothes, and I looked on while they rummaged through and spread the fabrics on the chair, admiring them. I could not hear a thing, only a heavy humming in my ears, as if I were sinking underwater.

Chapter six

I seriously considered fleeing home over the following days. But where to? I had nowhere to go and knew no one besides my friends. I would be brought back to the house by the end of the day if I fled to Oumi's or Fatima's house. I felt hopeless and trapped. I had no one to look to for advice; almost everyone in my family and among my family friends were in arranged marriages themselves, and this was all they knew. I had grown accustomed to the concept of arranged marriages, but still I was shaken that it was actually happening to me. I thought my life would be different; Aunty and Neneh had told me that I could do anything, that I could be whatever I wanted in my life. I felt betrayed. Batouly's silence and short comments exasperated me even more. "If you won't marry him, I will so he can take me to America. You're too stupid to even see how lucky you are," she said, her face blank as usual. Ousbi could not understand much of what was happening and why the whole thing made me sad, asking me if that wasn't what was supposed to happen anyway, his face sincere and innocent. He was more interested in hanging out with his friends and taking turns playing video games at Mr. Touré's house...I couldn't blame him. At least he was afforded the opportunity to paly games and not do chores because he was born a boy. I borrowed money from Fatima to go to the cybercafe to send an email to Koto.

Everything around me felt gloomy, and that gloominess must have been painted all over my face because after chemistry class that following week, Ms. Tawel asked me to stay behind. Fatima glanced at me while she gathered her belongings and left the classroom.

"What is the matter, Amina? Something is off with you," she said softly while fixing her eyes on me. I stayed quiet and looked down, fiddling with the hem of my skirt.

"Is something the matter at home?"

I remained quiet, and she did too, for a little while.

"Amina, I do not know what is happening to you, but I can tell that something is happening. I may not be able to help, but I can listen. Anything you say is safe with me, but if you are not comfortable..."

"They are going to marry me off!" I blurted out before she could finish her sentence. It was as if my body was waiting for this cue, because tears started uncontrollably running down my cheeks. I could not articulate my words as they got choked up before they could make it out of my mouth. Ms. Tawel got up and pulled me in for a hug while I sobbed. She let me cry, tapping me gently on the back until I could catch my breath again. When I pulled away, my tears had left a couple of wet spots on her white shirt.

"Here," she said, handing me a scarf that she pulled out of her bag. We remained silent for a moment longer while I dabbed the scarf on my face.

"I don't know what to do, Ms. Tawel, and I don't know why this is happening to me."

"I am sorry," she said softly as she rubbed my back again. I went on to tell her about the events of the prior weeks, occasionally sniffling in between sentences.

"I am totally against this practice, but I unfortunately live in a society where I, too, am limited in what I can do. I am really sorry, Amina, but as your teacher there is not much I can do; this is a family matter. Have you met him?"

"I have seen him briefly, but we have not talked yet. I will see him next Saturday."

"What were you first impressions of him? I mean, from

what you saw."

"Hmmm...I don't know.... He is young. My aunt told me that he lives in the US. That is where he studied."

"Oh, so he is not illiterate at least."

"I am told so," I answered.

She rubbed her cheek, pensive. "What do you want, Amina?"

I thought about it for a while. I had been so caught up in panic from the moment I had overheard that conversation that I had not taken the time to actually think.

"I don't know. I haven't really thought about it. I am just scared that I will not get to take my exams and go to university."

"The way I see it, if there is no way around it, it does not have to be all bad. The marriage will be between the two of you, and if he is a young guy who is educated, I imagine that maybe he is a sensible young man who can be talked to."

I looked at her, inquisitive.

"What I am saying is, since you are seeing him Saturday, you can maybe use that opportunity to gauge him. Try to find out what he is like, what his expectations are. Tell him yours, be candid, and tell him that you want to continue your studies. You will find out if that is something he is open to." She paused, stood up, walked to the door and back, then continued, "There are certain matters in our society that are difficult to go around. I have witnessed these things for so long, and it makes me sick that I am powerless. As I told you before. it is a family matter. But you do not have to be a pawn in a game; you can make it work so that you, too, get something out of it."

"But how?"

"Do you know if he intends on taking you to the US? Or is he planning on having a place mat wife who will live with his mother?"

"I do not know" I murmured.

"Find out! If he is planning on taking you with him to the US, then the silver lining for you is that you would have the opportunity to enroll in university there, but this will all depend on your assessment of him. So be smart, ask questions, listen carefully, and read between the lines."

"What if I say no, Ms. Tawel?"

"You could always say no, but there is no saying how your family would react, right? But even beyond that, you would just be kicking the can down the road, as someone else would inevitably show up to ask for your hand again sooner or later. What if he is worse? Illiterate? Maybe already married to a first wife?" I thought about it in horror. "We really do not know what the future holds— there may be someone better, or worse. Right now, you have to assess the current situation and see if you can make it work for you."

"Have you ever been married, Ms. Tawel?" The words came out unexpectedly. "I am sorry...I did not mean to..."

"Yes, I was, for a short period. Maybe I will tell you about it one day, but right now you need to get something to eat before your next class. Don't worry, and remember what I told you." I nodded as I left the classroom. Fatima was standing right outside, waiting for me with two fatayas and frozen ginger juice cones in hand. My stomach grumbled.

"She is not wrong, you know," Fatima said later between bites when I told her about the conversation. "Maybe you will even be able to come to Canada to live with me if it does not work out, and you may be able to send for your brothers. Remember Fatou Balde? She was not even in the US for five years when she filed for her mother and sisters. I think they all live in Atlanta now."

"Mmmm..." I mumbled, biting into my fataya, thoughts running through my head as I replayed the conversation with Ms. Tawel. Calculated. She was asking me to be calculated about the situation. This was definitely not how I had pictured getting married. I had always imagined meeting the man whom I would marry at university—maybe we would bump into each other while running to our classes like I saw in the movies. My papers would scatter around, and he would help me pick them up, apologizing profusely until we made that first eye contact. We would immediately be smitten with each other. We would get ice cream and be inseparable from that moment on. He would write me poems, help me with my papers. We would sometimes sneak out together at night and watch the stars in the sky while talking about our dreams.

He would be my best friend and my lover. I would invite him one afternoon to meet my family. He would have tea with Uncle on the terrace while Aunty and I gushed about him. How had I ever thought that any of that would even be possible? "How stupid!" I said out loud while Fatima looked at me with one of those what-the-hell-are-you-talking-about faces. We both laughed.

On a lazy afternoon marked by a soft breeze that almost imperceptibly moved the leaves of the tree in the courtyard, Uncle Abdul and my paternal uncles Oury and Alseny sat on a raffia mat under the mango tree, exchanging pleasantries. On the small charcoal stove, the teapot was boiling, and occasionally a few tea leaves escaped in a cluster of bubbles. Ousbi tended to the teapot and mechanically fanned the fire to revive the coals. Uncle had called for Aunty and me, and we both came out carrying wooden stools and sat to the side. I had received Koto's reply to my email earlier that day.

Dear Amina Bobo,
What news!! Knowing you, I am sure you are freaking out right now, so settle down a bit (smile). I have read and reread your message a thousand times, and I have been trying to come up with the words to give you the perfect answer, but I've realized that the best thing to say are words that come from my heart. This is indubitably a new chapter in your life.

69

While you may still be young, you are way more adult than I can ever claim to be. I have seen you grow and overcome obstacles like no one else. I know how scary this all may seem to you, but know that I have and will always have your back whatever direction you decide to go in.

Your brother who loves you very much.

I wished he had been present. I needed my koto in this time. After the endless formalities, Uncle started and addressed me.

"As you know, we have received a marriage proposal for you. They have not yet officially handed in the cola nuts, but it is as good as done. We have sought the advice from our close relatives and carefully considered it. We have now called for your paternal uncles to discuss, as the final decision is theirs," he said solemnly as he nodded in my paternal uncles' direction.

"He is an educated young man, he has good values, we know his family very well, and they are good people," he continued, but I had stopped listening. There was no longer any point in doing so. Aunty had pulled me to the back of the house earlier and begged me to abstain from speaking out and saying no. She gave a speech about protecting the family and placing traditions over emotions. "Do you want to be an outcast and bring shame to our family?" she asked with a veil of worry on her face. Because that was it—the girls who dared to say no were cast out by their families, the very families that were supposed to protect them; they were shunned by the community, labeled as dishonorable, disrespectful, and disobedient. My father's brother, Alseny, had walked by right at that moment and muttered, "She reads too much, this one," as he spat cola nut–tainted saliva on the gravel and limped away with a tea kettle in his hands, throwing his oversized boubou back on his shoulder. I was trapped. Trapped by tradition. Trapped by a flawed tradition and culture.

The dreaded Saturday finally arrived. He pulled up in the red Nissan. I was peering out of the bedroom window. Aunty had given me a new ankara outfit to wear, but it was ill fitting when I tried it on that morning, and it did not feel like me. So, I chose to wear my blue dress with black low-heel shoes. I looked out of the window again. I observed him get out of the car and shake Uncle's hand. He did not wear red pants this time. He was dressed in blue jeans, a white tee, and his white sneakers. I could not see their faces, but they had the demeanor of people in a good mood, chatting away without a care. My legs felt like cotton as I walked out when Aunty called my name. There were introductions, some laughs, and a little more pleasantry all while I fixed my shoes, wishing that I had worn different ones. I heard him asking Uncle for permission to take me out to a restaurant, and soon we were off.

I felt awkward riding next to him in the car, and I kept smoothing out my dress with my hands. I occasionally stole glimpses at him. He smelled of laundry detergent, a floral one; it must have been his crisp shirt. He was not bad looking. He looked fresh shaven, his nose was strong, his lips full, and he had extremely white teeth, almost unnatural. His fingers on the steering wheel were slender, and he occasionally released his grip to drum slightly to Sekouba Bambino playing on the radio. He drove us to a restaurant in Kipe. The restaurant was mostly frequented by foreigners who ordered colorful drinks with little umbrellas inside it. I had passed by it several times and often wondered what it would be like to sit on the terrace and nonchalantly order food, my own colorful little drink, and sit back. We did not go to restaurants; the closest I had been to eating in one was when we went to the blue tarp–covered shack by the school to order a huge plate of attiéké with braised fish and plantains whenever we had a little extra money.

We sat on the open terrace and observed the passersby silently for a moment. The waitress asking for our drink orders broke the silence.

"I will have a Coke, in a can please, if you have it. What will you have?" he asked, looking at me.

"I will have the same," I answered.

"Do you what you want to eat so we can order now?" he said.

"Hmm...I do not know."

"I will bring you the menus shortly," the waitress chimed in and walked away.

"So, you go by Amina, huh…" He smiled at me.

"Yes, short for Aminatou. Do you go by Boubacar?"

"Yes, at work and with acquaintances, it is Boubacar; but with family and friends, I go by Bouba." He fiddled with the napkin on the table. "I know this must be strange…" He started but did not finish his sentence. The waitress came back with the menus.

"Oh, I already know what I want—I will get the wings with fries, and some spicy sauce on the side." His voice was almost flat and monotone whenever he spoke. I looked at the menu a little longer not knowing what to order, and I decided on a shawarma.

"Would you like that with chicken or beef?" the waitress inquired. She tilted her head when she talked, and the side of her mouth scrunched up in a grimace.

"Beef please," I replied, wondering what was wrong with her face. I watched her walk away, apprehensive of being alone with him again.

"So, tell me about you, Amina. What do you like to do?" He leaned in, joining his hands and interlocking his fingers on the table.

"How do you know about me?" I asked, barely leaving him time to finish his sentence.

"Okaayy…" he laughed. "Not exactly an answer, but okay. Well, I did not know about you until recently, and by that, I mean a couple of weeks ago when I arrived. My mother has been searching for a potential wife for me, and from what I understand, she knew your mother well."

"She did?" I knew that his mother sometimes visited Aunty and Uncle, but I did not think she actually knew my mother.

"Yes, they apparently worked together at the bauxite company back in the day."

"Oh, I see."

"So, she has known you since you were little. She only has great things to say about you. The man I came with the other day is my father's brother. He knew your parents, too."

"Yes, I got that part," I muttered.

"I don't really know how this works, but my mom made the choices for me, and she showed me some pictures when I arrived. That is how we ended up coming over to your house last time," he added. I raised an eyebrow.

"Just like that?"

"Well, yes and no. There are other factors, too, and I did ask her to only introduce me to girls who are educated and over eighteen. I understand you graduate high school this year?"

"Yes, but I am not quite eighteen yet," I answered dryly.

"But soon." He smiled again. I did not want to admit it, but he was not an unpleasant person.

"I take it you are okay with this then?" I asked him, scrutinizing his face.

"Look, Amina, this is not how I saw things going for me. I have been away for a few years, and I have a little different outlook on life; however, my family has been hounding me for the past four years to get married. Not to just anyone, but to someone of their choosing. I love my parents and deeply respect them. They have done everything for me, and I will do whatever it takes to make them happy, even if that means I have to let go of something I really want. You know how these things go..." He trailed of. "I am sure that this is not the ideal scenario you had pictured, either, but if you are willing, we can find a way to make this work." He leaned back and took his turn in scrutinizing me.

"How? Why me?" I asked back, inquisitive.

"I'll be honest, you were not the only one my mother picked for me, but something drew me to you."

"From a picture? Really?" I said, my tone snarky. "How did she get my picture anyway?" I already knew the answer to that question. He paused for a few seconds before answering.

"Yes, from a picture. She must have gotten it from your aunt, but something about you was different, and I am starting to see it." I rolled my eyes internally. "To answer your question as to how we could make this work, I do not have a specific answer for you, but I believe that if we are both willing to try and put some effort into it, then maybe it can work." The whole thing felt like a business transaction, impersonal. When was the waitress bringing the food? she thought.

"I would like to get to know you, Amina, and I hope you are open to getting to know me, too. One thing I do want to say is that I am not looking for someone to cook and clean for me. I have been doing that for myself for the past eight years. What I need is a partner. I get from what everyone is telling me that you are smart and have always been at the top of your class. I am not looking to take you away from that. I would like a wife who is as educated as me, so if your wish is to continue your studies, I have no reservations about it, and I will help you in that direction. That is the reason why I asked my mother for an educated girl. If for any reason you feel like I am not someone you could see yourself with, then I will ask my parents to withdraw the proposal." I thought that my ears were deceiving me. Maybe I was imagining a completely different conversation in an alternate dimension. Should I slap myself? Because this was definitely not what I thought I would hear from someone like him. Someone who was at peace with marrying a total stranger, someone who relied on his parents to pick a total stranger to be his lawfully wedded wife. I imagined he would be abrupt, unyielding, entitled. I was astonished.

"Is that something you want? I guess I should ask: What do you want, Amina?" His voice brought me back out of my head. No, I was not dreaming. Everything seemed to light up at once for me. His voice sounded less monotone and achromatic. The signs on the pharmacy across the street seemed a little greener and fluorescent to me; the tie-dye crop top of the girl crouched against a pole selling coconuts seemed a whole lot more colorful. Had those flowers always been there on the table? How beautiful they were. My life outlook seemed less bleak as soon as those words rolled out of his mouth without my even asking. The food came, and it was delectable. My ears perked up, ready to take in more. I learned that he was twenty-nine, an engineer working for a company in Washington, DC. He studied at the University of Maryland. His parents had used up all their savings and relationships to get him there. It had been a struggle for him, and it took him six years to finish his degree. He worked nights in a warehouse and went to school part time in the afternoons. He played soccer on Saturday mornings with a small league of players he had met when he was an international student. His favorite dish was cassava leaves cooked with palm oil, and he loved Bob Marley and mystery TV shows. Maybe this didn't have to be all bad. Ms. Tawel's words resonated again in my ears. Maybe what was supposed to be my doom would turn out to be my solace.

Bouba's family officially asked for my hand with a bundle of cola nuts two weeks later. I saw him thrice more since that day at the restaurant. We talked and walked around the neighborhood, and I was starting to get accustomed to his presence; his soft chuckle; his unidimensional, measured voice; and his long strides when he walked. I convinced myself that I was getting used to those things. There were several more meetings with his family and mine. Koto was conferenced in for some of them. He could not attend the ceremony as the plane ticket was expensive, and he could not get away from the job he had just started. He spoke to Bouba on the phone and gave his blessings.

The families wanted the marriage ceremony to take place right away to ensure that the union remained pure, so the wedding was set for the last Friday of the lunar month before Ramadan, which was in exactly three weeks, right after my exams in June. It was no coincidence that marriage inquiries started around that period. Many young women are married off during this time as the month leading to Ramadan is believed to bring prosperity to the couple and also their families, and most important, the new bride is set on a stage to show her skills and worthiness as new housewife, attending to her new husband and his family, strengthening her relationship with God, and preparing the fast-breaking meals all while fasting. That whole month was decked with ceremonies and blushing brides—it was a peak wedding time.

Chapter Seven

The baccalauréat was rough. A week of exams, intense and stressful in a packed, sweltering hot center in Yimbayah. The unfamiliar setting of the testing center threw me off on the first day, and as if that was not enough, my period decided to rear its head ahead of schedule. I was unprepared, and all we were allowed to carry into the center were a pencil and a badge. In a panic, I ran to the lady selling oranges outside the gates, not knowing exactly what she could do for me; I meekly told her that my monthly visitor had come early and that I needed something. Without a word, she walked me a couple of houses down, where she motioned for me to follow her inside. She tore off a piece a cloth out of a wrap and handed it to me. "This is all I can do for you; I do not have the fancy stuff," she said, referring to menstruation pads. Heroes come in all shapes and forms. I found my cadence soon enough and drilled through the subjects while the exam proctor paced up and down the aisles. At the end of the day, I met up with Fatima who had been assigned to a different testing center, and we went over the exam questions while riding back to her house to study until late evening before heading back to mine. My house was too animated at the time, as the wedding was right around the corner. I felt completely detached from everything; it was as if it were someone else's wedding. I tried to feel excited and hoped to conjure up some feelings as it got closer, but it was in vain. Maître Talib, the tailor, was in charge of making my wedding dress. Aunty had chosen a sparkly white bazin fabric that would be embroidered with golden threads. He had carefully taken my measurements while I stood rigid in the middle of his workshop, and we spent a couple of hours peering through catalogs to pick the perfect model that he would recreate.

The house was buzzing with activity. Bags of potatoes, rice, corn, beans, onions, twenty-liter cans of vegetable oil, and boxes of condensed Gloria milk for the kossam all fought for space in the kitchen and hallways in preparation for the festivities. A cow was brought in, and it peacefully grazed on the grass in the back of the house, blissfully unaware that it was waiting to be turned into barbecue. The distant aunts had started coming out of the woods and moved into the house, where they would stay until the wedding was over. They talked and cackled late into the night, taking up all the space in our cushy beds, while Batouly and I slept on the floor. I woke up with aches and pains and was groggy all day. School was over, and we were now waiting for the exam results to be released, so I did not have any place to escape to, and I awaited our school trip to Kamsar that weekend with impatience. I asked Aunty for permission to spend a couple of nights at Fatima's house, giving her upcoming voyage to Canada as a pretext, but more than anything, I needed to get away from the house and all the brouhaha. Fatima had received her visa and would be traveling in a month. A little piece of paper placed in her passport. A little piece of paper that looked insignificant but that carried so much weight. It had all become too real. I was going to be separated from my best friend, and I was getting married to a stranger. We lay on our sides those couple of nights, face to face in her bed, using our hands as pillows and talking all night until we heard the roosters crow at the crack of dawn.

The weekend following the end of the baccalauréat was a celebration—a celebration of the end of the examinations and the long years of preparation. The tradition was that the entire class would take a trip to a destination chosen by the school director at the beginning of the year. The prior year's destination was the city of Kindia, and this year, we were going to Kamsar. I did not know much about the city; the only thing I knew was that my mother had gone there and never came back. A lot of strings had been pulled to get her into the Kamsar hospital, which was one of the best at the time, but she still had not made it. I had mixed feelings about it, but regardless, I was excited about the trip and to get away from my life, even if it was just for a weekend.

Two buses rented for the occasion were parked at the entrance of the school, and we lined up on the side, waiting for our names to be called to board. The excitement was palpable. We were all animated and forgot for the time being that the exam results had still not been released yet. We did not care in that moment. Fatima and I chose seats in the back of the bus when we were called upon to board, and I took the seat closest to the window. Mamady and Oumi sat across the aisle from us. Fatima's mom had made us sandwiches for the road, as well as some bissap juice, frozen in a mineral water bottle. We set the bag aside for later and partook in the hubbub happening around us. My cousin Aziz was coming along on the trip, too. He was not in our class but had been given a waiver by the administration because it was his only year at the school, and he would soon be returning to France for his last year of high school. He was sitting with a group of boys near the front, bantering. They had stopped making fun of his French accent and the way he rolled his Rs or the guttural sound he made when his words came out of his throat. The teachers and chaperones took the first two rows of seats and completed one last head count before the bus slowly pulled away. The tumult died down after an hour. We still had two and a half hours to go, so the buses stopped midway for a road break. Some of the boys ran into the bushes to relieve themselves. I stepped off the bus and took in a deep breath as I stretched my arms, forming a V in the air; already, the air was fresher. The road stretched ahead and was surrounded by tall grasses on both sides. Some of the students were sitting on the side of the road, unpacking their snacks and lunches. Fatima emerged of the bus with the plastic bag filled with food.

We all gathered our things when rain started sprinkling and found our way back to our individual seats. The driver started the bus, which made a rattling sound as it got back on the road. I wondered what would happen if the bus were to suddenly break down. I erased the thought from my head; nothing could ruin this weekend for me. The second part of the trip was much quieter. It must have been the boiled yams, fatayas, and bean-filled sandwiches weighing down their bellies, but most of the students on the bus were asleep. I could feel the vibrations of the bus under my feet. It was soothing, and it was also making me sleepy. I had managed to only get three hours of sleep the night before. I tried hard not to doze off, fearing that it would put me in a deep slumber and drain all the energy out of me. I tried to focus on the scenery, but beyond the lush greenery and occasional village in the distance, the view was limited. The raindrops on my window quickly pearled up and slowly disintegrated as they rolled down the glass, and I tried to trace them with my finger against the glass on the other side. I hoped the rain would clear up before we arrived.

Soon, the huts became more frequent, then the huts were replaced by houses, which then became denser along the road. I could see a big factory silhouette forming slowly through the cloudy and rainy weather. On the side of the street, peddlers ran to cars that were pulling over, trying to sell rice cakes, warm soda cans, or boiled cassava. A couple of decades back, Kamsar had been just a tiny fishing village in the middle of nowhere until the Americans came and installed a bauxite mining operation. It was now a bustling port city, our teacher Mr. Kourouma told us, and it housed a company that was one of the largest bauxite exporters in the world. As we got closer, the houses became nicer, the lines cleaner, the roads smoother, and the hedges more symmetrical, but they still all looked like they had been sprinkled with red dust. I was amazed at what I was seeing; I felt like we had stepped into a different world.

It took over an hour to get everyone checked in to the hotel. There were four of us in our room, sharing two queen-size beds. Fatima threw our things on one of the beds before we headed back out to the lobby for the scheduled guided tour of the city. It only took us two hours to drive around the small city, making occasional stops for our guide to give us details about the sites we were visiting. There was not a lot to see, but still, the community was captivating, likable, and organized, unlike the chaos of Conakry. All the neighborhoods had names, and the houses were numbered in an alphabetical and numerical order starting with villa A1. The A homes housed the top executives of the company, our guide told us. The further you got down the alphabet, the smaller and barer the houses became. In the neighborhood with letters higher in the alphabet, I mostly saw foreigners. They walked peacefully, rode bikes, and played tennis and basketball in the different corners of their neighborhood. In the X and Y neighborhoods, flowers were sparser, clothes hung on lines, and children with protruding bellies played in the streets. The setup somewhat reminded me of our home in Simbayah. All the Russian workers lived in a separate area of the big compound. Their basketball and tennis courts were surrounded by tall wire fences, and every so often, we could see guards chasing the kids who had trespassed on the courts. It made Koto angry. We drove past the hospital on the way to the port, and I looked the other way. I did not want to see it as I feared that it would be all I would remember from the trip. By the time we finished dinner in the hall that was reserved for us, I could barely keep my eyelids open, so I excused myself and headed to bed while the other students counted the money they had so they could buy ice cream at a parlor we had seen earlier nearby. I had not thought about what was happening back home all day. I felt relaxed and happy, and I replayed the day in my head as I slowly drifted off to sleep with a smile on my face.

The next day, humongous excavating machines rolled down the open pit in front of our eyes. They seemed almost minuscule in the massiveness of the hole. The haul ramp that was dug into the side of the pit formed a continuous loop into the crater. We were at one of the three Bauxite mines.

"Our country holds the world's largest bauxite reserves!" Mr. Kourouma boasted. "Don't you ever wonder why the ground you walk on is so red? It is because the bauxite deposits are found almost at the earth's surface. They do not even have to dig deep; it is lying right there just a couple of meters below the surface," he said, stomping his foot two times as if to make his point. "The mined minerals are carried by truck from the different mines to the refining factory we visited yesterday, then loaded onto ships at the port to be exported and transformed into aluminum."

"If only they would reinvest some of the profits in the rural lands they are destroying!" Ms. Tawel yelled from the back. Mr. Kourouma frowned at her and resumed his lecture. Most of the students were uninterested.

We couldn't wait to go to lunch because all the walking and the hot sun had worn us out and dug a hole in our stomachs that could rival the pit we had just seen; but mostly, we couldn't wait to head to our final stop on our way back to Conakry, the Bel Air Beach.

We all hurried through lunch because the sooner we were done, the sooner we would be on our way to the beach. We all sat on benches under a large tarp and waited for sandwiches and water cones that were being distributed. I sat next to Ms. Tawel. She was wearing her usual white shirt, khaki pants, and fierce Afro. I wanted to have a conversation with her, and I wanted to seem curious and interested in something important, so I asked, "What did you mean earlier, Ms. Tawel, about destroying the rural lands?" She looked at me for a moment before answering.

"Someone was listening!" she said, grinning at me. I smiled, feeling proud. She put down her sandwich in the paper plate before continuing, "You see, although the mining activities provide thousands of jobs to the locals, they have deep consequences for the rural communities that live in the vicinity of the mining operations." She went on to explain how the mining company was in a joint venture with the government, but that the government just pocketed its part of the profits, which ended up in corrupt officials' bank accounts. She explained how the mining companies took advantage of the lack of protection for rural lands to expropriate ancestral farmlands with the help of the government, and without adequate compensation—the financial payments the villagers received were so meager that they could never surmount the benefits they would have derived from the land. Once the windfall was spent, most of the farmers were left without sustainable sources of income in the long term because very few of them were qualified to obtain jobs at the mining company. I listened to her intently. The mining activities also produced a residue that fell every evening after the factory shut down, like a shower of red dust, which covered everything and blended in with the breathing air. That explained the layers of red dirt I saw on the flowers, the cars, the roofs, and the chairs outside the hotel. Damage was also done to water resources, which were becoming more and more scarce, so the women in the surrounding villages had to wake up earlier and walk longer to get to a potable water source. I listened in shock. I had asked just to make conversation, but I was appalled by what Ms. Tawel was telling me. Our discussion was interrupted by Mr. Kourouma's whistle, signaling us to assemble for boarding. For a short while, I had forgotten about the beach, but now the excitement reemerged. I had to tell Fatima about my conversation with Ms. Tawel.

We finally arrived at the beach. The buses stopped on the last main road as they couldn't drive any farther because of the vegetation and sinuous path; so, we walked the rest of the way, crossing a small village with a few tiny straw huts sparsely scattered around. The smell of the sea hit my nostrils, and I knew we were getting close. There were hundreds of coconuts and palm trees, and the ground was no longer red but a faded beige clay. We crossed a clearing, and all of a sudden, there it was in all its majesty. The ocean lay in front of us, shimmering under the sunlight, blue, infinite, and beautiful. It was starkly different from the murky and smelly waters on the banks of the ocean in Conakry. I took a deep breath of fresh air and opened my arms. Fatima and Oumi pulled their pant legs to their knees and ran into the water, followed by a group of screaming students. I followed suit.

The warm waves crashed against my ankles, and the white sand escaped between my toes, sending a pleasant sensation through my whole body. Mr. Kourouma and the rest of the teachers also stepped into the water, smiles painted all over their faces. There were a few bungalows nearby, and part of the group walked toward them to probably change into their swimming suits. Joy took over my body. I suddenly felt light, light like the birds flying above our heads. I laughed at the slightest things all afternoon and grabbed every occasion to run back into the water in a splash of glee. When Fatima and I rested later, lazily spread out on the sand, I felt calm and peaceful. I had never felt so calm and peaceful despite all the ruckus around me. I took it all in and engraved the memory in my brain forever. I wished we could stay on that beach for eternity, but eventually, it was time to start walking back to the buses. My mood shifted at the thought of getting back to the reality of my life. As if in anticipation of an impact, my body stiffened. With every step I took, a knot formed inside my belly, anxiety crept up further into my chest, and my breath became shallower.

Chapter Eight

The wedding day came. One can set a date as far or as close as one wishes, but once it is set, its arrival is a certainty. I had often heard the saying, but now I felt the saying. The women had cooked until very late in the night and were up again at dawn to finish up the meals, which were arranged in the dining room in innumerable serving dishes. They barely had time to shower the grease and tar from the wood fire off of their bodies before it was dressing time. Ousbi and the neighborhood boys had spent the whole morning sweeping the whole compound, sprinkling water to settle the dust, and arranging the rented chairs and tables around, while two women set up the newlyweds' seating areas under the white tent. I spent the late morning at the salon with Fatima, Oumi, Aunty, and an army of women all waiting to be done up. It was a deafening cacophony of voices. There was makeup everywhere, head wraps, accessories, and hair extensions for chignons as the salon girls hurried around to get everyone ready in time.

The religious ceremony went on without a hitch. All the men of the family—the groom, neighbors, and other guests—had joined the imam of the mosque for the two-o'clock prayer, and afterward they prayed and gave blessings over the mound of colas that were wrapped in brown paper and tied with rope, with the dowry on the side, to seal the union. It was said that the tighter the knots of the rope, the stronger the union would be. After the men returned, there was singing, dancing, and food, so much food. Bouba and I were seated on a throne-like loveseat. It had a white satin sheet thrown over it, and it was decorated with flowers and a big white-and-pink tulle bow. I had not seen him in a couple of days. He was dressed in white bazin caftan, also embroidered with golden threads around the collar and down the center of his garment. He wore a golden Fez hat and new white babouches. I could not read his face but did not have time to scrutinize him because there was a line of people waiting to take pictures with the new couple. One should be able to remember their wedding, but the whole day had been a blur—sequences of moments, people dancing, others eating, others discarding their empty plates and cans of soda under their chairs, griots singing praises of guests in the hopes of scoring a few bank notes.

At sundown, the women of his family came to fetch me. I was led to the bedroom where I was seated on a brand-new wooden stool purchased for the occasion, and my feet were washed with fresh water in a calabash. Then my hands and my face. The women of his family had brought the new bride outfit—a white wrap for my body and another to put over my head like a veil. My uncle came into the room then to give the traditional speech before they took me away.

You are now a married woman, and you are going into a new family that will be yours from this day on. Your husband is the head and guardian of the family. One of your chief duties as a wife toward your husband is to obey him in everything that is not unlawful. It is also your duty to guard your honor and that of your husband, to pray your five daily prayers, to fast the month of Ramadan, and to attend to the affairs of your house. May Allah bless your union.

There was more singing followed by an exchange of gifts that took a whole hour, each family trying to outdo the other. Night had fallen, and the music had already died down when we came out of the house. The guests had slowly scattered, and women were packing leftover food in any containers they could find to take home with them. A barrage of cousins and friends with Fatima at the head suddenly appeared from nowhere, demanding that dues be paid before they let their bride go—one last ritual of the bride's family before their girl went into another family, for good. His family, evidently prepared, started dishing out bank notes, to the elation of the group. We soon found ourselves at the gate waiting for the driver to pull up the car that would drive us to his parent's house—me, Bouba's mother, and a couple of his aunts. I was distracted and lost in my thoughts about what was to come. I remember being hugged and squeezed by a procession of friends, cousins, and aunts who bequeathed last-minute wisdoms that I cannot recall, the car getting loaded with suitcases and gifts, and someone helping me up into the car. The car ride was silent. I stared at my hands, wondering where Bouba was. I could not decipher my own feelings. I both dreaded and looked forward to being alone with him. I had often imagined being with a man for the first time, but I was perplexed as to what would happen. I froze at the thought that I actually had no idea of what to do when we found ourselves alone, in a bedroom. I had had many giggle-filled whispers with Fatima and Oumi, mostly speculations of what sex would be like. I secretly read *Cosmopolitan* magazines that we passed around between classes, and more than often daydreamed about Andre, my high school crush, but our experiments as a group never went beyond a shy peck on the lips and an occasional furtive breast squeeze behind a stairwell. Sex was not a topic I could bring up to anyone around me, the subject being so taboo. I swallowed hard and felt panic.

"We are here, madame." The driver's voice sounded far away. The car came to a stop. I looked out the car window. We were in front of a small yellow building with green shutters and adorned with flower beds. The patio had white tiles with a couple of bamboo chairs in the corner, and it was filled with plants potted in clay pots. Some of them hung from the ceiling, spilling their leaves outward. Bouba was standing with a few of his friends at the bottom of the steps. He started walking toward the car.

"We are here, my dear," said his mother. "Come on, let's go," she added to me as she got out of the car. The aunts came out of the car, and Bouba's sister Bijou stepped up to me, took me by the hand, and started walking me toward a coconut tree in the front yard. I was perplexed for a second until I remembered that Aunty had told me about this. The young woman walked me around the tree three times while Bouba's oldest aunt watched. The ritual required the groom's sister to walk the new bride around a tree that bore fruit before entering the house for the very first time. This would help the new couple to have a fruitful and fertile marriage. I climbed the steps slowly, and my dress felt heavy. The rest of Bouba's family had arrived before us, and they welcomed us with some songs and dance. I couldn't take it anymore. After what seemed to be an eternity, they finally stopped and bid us good night. Bouba's mother welcomed me to the house and asked me to call her Neneh, as she was now my Neneh. No one will ever replace my Nene, I thought as I watched her walk upstairs holding on to the rails and her grand boubou. I stood still in the middle of the living room, unsure of what to do. Bouba walked up to me and said, "I have a small apartment in the back of the house that I use when I am here. Come on, let's go." And we walked out of the back door through the kitchen.

I felt panic as we entered the small house, which was almost bare except for a sofa, a table, dinette, TV, and small fridge. A painting hung above the TV.

"Are you alright?" Bouba asked me. I mumbled something.

"Welcome! This is my place. Our place..." There was a knock on the door, and then the driver came in lugging bags.

"Put them in the bedroom please, down the hallway. I was saying, this is our temporary abode, until you obtain a visa. We will start the procedures right away." He took off his Fez hat and continued, "You know, I will have to leave before you." He slumped into the small couch.

"Oh, why is that?"

"Well...work, I have used up all the time I had and even borrowed some. I did not expect to be out here this long. I also need to plan your arrival. Why are you standing there? Come sit next to me."

I shyly made my way to the sofa and sat at the edge.

"I only get fifteen days of paid time off a year. I had accumulated some from prior years and added some compensatory time, which is why I have been able to stay this long. I have used it all up, and I need to get back to work."

"Paid time off?" I asked, perplexed. He laughed a hearty belly laugh.

"You will understand when you come to America." That was the first time I saw him laugh like that. He looked like he did not have a care in the world in that moment. I wanted to feel like that. My stomach grumbled. I realized I was starving; I had barely eaten all day, having a dozen pair of eyes staring at me, and I had not touched the food they had served us during the ceremony.

"Is there any food? I am hungry."

"Me too. With all that food that was served today, I do not think I even had a bite, and it was our party!" he laughed. "Maybe the driver can get us a couple of shawarmas around the corner." He turned the TV on, leaned back, and let out a long sigh.

I stood up. "I am going to take a shower."

"The bathroom is down the hall, next to the bedroom."

"Okay, I won't be long." I turned to leave. He nodded and flipped the channel.

The bedroom was simple but nice, with white curtains and floral bedding. The bed sat in the center, flanked with nightstands on both sides, with a lamp in the corner. The air conditioner hummed quietly. After fighting with my dress to get out of it, I stood for a moment and realized that my hands were shaking. I took a deep breath to calm my nerves. The bathroom too was simple and clean. There was a small square area for the shower, a white ceramic toilet, a sink that had some toiletries, and a razor and a toothbrush scattered on it. A black plastic pail full of water sat under a faucet in the corner. I turned the shower dial, stepping onto the ceramic floor. I was pleasantly surprised to find out that the water coming out of the showerhead was warm. The last time I had taken a warm shower was in our home in Simbayah. The warm droplets of water rolled onto my skin and felt appeasing. I closed my eyes and forgot everything for a heavenly moment.

After coming out of the bathroom, I searched the pile of luggage for the little carry-on that my friends had packed for me for my first night. There was a panoply of things...I took a breath. My shaky hands gravitated toward a pink satin robe that I put on. I looked at my reflection in the mirror, stared back at my brown eyes, gazed at my dark brown skin and my full lips. My natural curls had been hot combed and coiffed into a chignon for the wedding ceremony. I turned sideways and wished that my hips were fuller and curvier like Fatima's and less like the almost-boyish figure I had. "This is it, Amina," I said to myself. I felt my legs get shaky, so I sat on the bed and took deep breaths until I felt calm enough. I must have been gone a long time, because when I stepped out into the small living room, Bouba was fast asleep, remote in hand, two Coca-Cola cans and two shawarmas laid out on a plate on the coffee table.

We did not consummate our marriage on our wedding night, or the following nights. I felt relief and angst at the same time. "Let's not rush; we have a lifetime ahead of us," he had wittingly said the next morning. He did not mention the previous night, but I knew what he was alluding to. "Umm...and let's keep it between us, yeah?" he added hesitantly. "You know, this is between the two of us, and no one else needs to know...right? We will do things in our own time. We do not need someone to dictate things for us." I looked down and nodded my head.

The week after the wedding was filled with family visits, both his and mine. We had to personally make the rounds and thank all our uncles, aunts, cousins, and other relatives that our respective families had put on "the list." When we got back to the apartment, there was a parade of friends bringing gifts, food, or "checking on us," which kept us occupied sometimes late into the night. I dodged the occasional wedding night questions by looking away, feigning shyness, and changing the subject. How distasteful, I thought. Who asks those types of questions anyway? I did not understand how my wedding night was anyone's business. I was just overjoyed when I found out that Bouba's family, after prolonged discussions with him, had decided at his request to forego the long-held tradition of the virginity check, when the old ladies sat outside the newlyweds' bedroom door on the wedding night, waiting for the groom to hand them the nuptial sheets so they could inspect it for bloodstains, attesting to the bride's virginity and purity. I shuddered at the thought of it. Not because I had secrets, but the sheer idea of having such a private, intimate moment violated by prying eyes made me nauseous. The stories of girls rejected by their new spouse, girls who had brought shame to their families and were dragged out by their groom's family, were an all-too-familiar cautionary tale.

I welcomed the busyness and constant hum because it kept the questions at bay. In the quiet moments, when he was fast asleep next to me and snoring, I was overcome by feelings of inadequateness. Why hadn't he touched me, or even attempted to? Was he not attracted to me? Then why go through all of this? He was gentle and attentive, he sometimes held my hand, and even once he gently rubbed my back while I laid on the couch; but whenever it was time to go to bed, he gave me a soft kiss, wished me good night, and turned to face the wall. "Maybe he can't get it up," Fatima had suggested, when after the first three nights I couldn't take it anymore and had to confide in someone. "You know it happens; I have heard of these types of things happening." Oumi's theory was that maybe he was gay and had gotten married just to appease his family and bury suspicions. She had also heard of stories like that. I took that thought in with horror for a minute, and then rejected it. They both suggested I make a move, but I was terrified. How would I even do that? What if he rejected me?

"Don't worry about that; we will go and see Aunty Finda," Oumi said, laughing and winking at Fatima. Aunty Finda was an older woman who sat in a dark corner of the Cosa market in a makeshift boudoir. She taught the art of seduction to women, young and middle aged, who were looking to lure in potential suitors or wandering husbands, and she sold items referred to as "Secrets de Femmes"—women's secrets. She shared special recipes, seductive accessories, alluring gestures, and foolproof actions to women to entice men to enter their secret garden and travel to the heavens of bliss. "A woman must have more than one trick up her sleeve," Oumi whispered in my ear as she brushed past me, smiling mischievously. I considered it for a moment, then decided against it. Just the thought of it made my heart want to jump out of my chest and my hands clammy.

Bouba bought me a Nokia phone so that he could call me directly after he left. I stared and played with it for hours. Not many people owned cell phones, so it was a collective luxury for the household. Besides my clothing and books, I had never owned anything, and that phone was my most valuable possession. I rushed to charge it every time the power came back, hiding it behind a pile of books. Before long, it was Bouba's last night in Conakry. He was set to fly back to Maryland the next day. We spent the day organizing all the paperwork he had brought in preparation for my potential visa interview, along with the ones we had printed from the corner cybercafe when he filled out the immigrant visa application. We spent a couple of hours filling out a tiresome long form with unusual words like *alien*, *petitioner*, *beneficiary*. It made me snicker a little. There was an endless list of papers to provide—copies of tax returns, civil documents, police reports, proof of employment, bank statements, an affidavit of support. "What is all this for?" I asked Bouba.

"They want to make sure that you will not smooch off the welfare system if accorded a visa, but mainly, it is because they want to make the process as daunting as possible to discourage people."

"What else would they like? Your grandma's bones?" I said, laughing. He laughed, too. It was the first time we had shared a laugh, and it felt good.

"I am telling you, getting into the US is no joke, and the media makes it sound like all these immigrants are just walking in, when the majority of people have to go through all this hassle of a process. If the leaders in this country were not so corrupt, and they could provide us with the basic necessities like water, power, health care, and good schools, who would need to go to America?" he said, almost resigned. I nodded, thinking that we were not there yet, far from it, and therefore America and its likes were a welcome boon for those who wanted something different.

"I may have to send you up-to-date pay stubs and bank statements once your visa date is confirmed. These will probably be out of date by the time your appointment comes around. Put these in a separate folder." He handed me a stack of papers. "I will forward you the link to check the status of the immigrant petition online." I nodded. It was all too much, too fast—but I went along.

That night, when I lay in bed, waiting to fall asleep, I was surprised to feel his hand on my body, timid at first, but increasingly confident and thirsty for more. My body stiffened as he got closer to me, and his need visibly became more urgent. I felt pain as he pushed through me and the weight of his body bore down on me. I went through the motions with him, awkward, raw, and uneasy. He reached climax, pulled away, and walked to the bathroom. A million thoughts were flying through my head. Was this what it was supposed to feel like? Was this how it was always going to feel? I did not experience any of the pleasure that I had heard came with sex. Was is because of my excision, I wondered. I felt sore and naked, both literally and figuratively. When he came out of the bathroom, he had an expression on his face that I could not read.

"There was no blood," he finally said when he had laid back down next to me. I looked at him in shock. I was in shock because this was contrary to everything he had claimed to be about. He had stood up to his mother to forego the virginity check, so what did it matter? I had once read a magazine at the French cultural center that said not all women bleed the first time they have intercourse. In fact, some hymens are so thin that they can break quite easily before a woman even has a sexual encounter. A lack of blood after the first intercourse did not necessarily mean lost virginity. I wanted to hurl those words at him, but I couldn't speak. My ears hummed and my heart rate increased. I felt groundlessly judged, affronted, and shamed. I stormed into the bathroom and locked the door. I fought back the tears, but I could not control them as they came rushing out of my eyes in a stream, rolling down my cheeks and onto my lips, salty and bitter.

He left the next day. He handed me an envelope of bank notes before we left for the airport to cover my expenses, and another to his mother. Our goodbyes were dry and awkward. He called three days after he left, and every couple of days after that. He spoke lengthily to his mother before hanging up and calling me on my Nokia. Our conversations were brief and devoid of meaning. That was my marriage. My relationship was limited to quick, scheduled phone calls with a man I did not know how I felt about; all I knew was that whenever I thought back to that last evening with him, I felt hollow inside.

Chapter Nine

I was serving lunch to my mother-in-law when I received the call from Fatima. I still wasn't used to having a phone with me wherever I went, and the ringing startled me. The baccalauréat results had been posted at the school, and she was on her way to pick me up. My hands shook as I lifted the ladle of fish soup, spilling a couple of drops on the tablecloth. I put a couple of spoonsful of rice on my plate, but I could not eat any longer, and I stared at the plate in front of me.

"Won't you eat before your food gets cold?" my mother-in-law asked, looking at me fiddling with the spoon.

"I am not very hungry, Neneh." I paused before continuing. "The exam results have been posted at the school. Fatima is on her way to pick me up to go look at the results."

"At last. It is taking them longer and longer nowadays to release exam results," she said, chewing on her food. "Well, eat something then before you go on." I tried eating a spoonful, but it was tasteless in my mouth. "I think I will save it for later. I am going to get ready."

"Don't be silly; if you won't eat it now, give it to the gateman."

I excused myself from the table and headed out with my plate in hand. Mamadou, the gateman, was sitting by the water faucet, supervising a group of girls fetching water. He did not wait for me to call him; he started walking my way as soon as he saw me with the plate. Mamadou never said no to an extra plate of food, even after he ate his large bowl of rice. Anyone who couldn't finish their food just called for him to get the food off their hands. It was a wonder how skinny he was.

Fatima arrived not long after. The driver honked a couple of times outside the gates, and I grabbed my phone and coin purse to head out. Our ride was much less chatty than usual, each one of us buried in our thoughts and a disquietude over the anticipation of knowing for certain if we had passed. There was a group of students in front of the posting board when we arrived at the school, and a girl in tears was sitting on the ground, being consoled by her friends. I felt a knot in my stomach. I stopped and told Fatima to check for me because I couldn't look. She grabbed me by the hand and pulled me forcefully, fraying a passage for us through the group. The list was blurry. I looked but I couldn't see; the words danced in front me, and I felt like I was going to pass out until I heard Fatima's squeal. My ear rang as she grabbed me and started jumping. "We made it! We made it! We are right there at the top." I believed her, but I had to see. I squinted my eyes at the list again, starting at the top, and sure enough, there it was. My name in black and white. I was right there, after Mohamed Fofana, second in the whole school, followed by Fatou Kaba, then Fatima. I felt a weight lift off my chest, and air could flow through my lungs again. I felt Fatima snatching my shirt from the back, still screaming. I had passed my exam. I felt exaltation for a moment, then remembered that we needed to check the board again for Mamady and the science board for Oumi. They had not yet arrived. They, too, had passed. What a great day it was. We stayed at the school for a couple of hours, looking over the list again to check the rankings of the entire class, talking, almost shouting, in excitement. The door to our future education was now wide open. I was still high from the excitement when Bouba called that night. I had forgotten for a brief moment that I was giving him the cold shoulder. We talked a little longer than usual, before I passed the phone to his mother.

The chaos and the heat in the airport parking lot were dizzying. It was crowded, and it smelled musty, a mix of perspiration, cheap perfumes, and clothes that had been sweated on and left in armoires for too long. There were the people traveling, but there were also the dozens of friends and relatives who had come to say goodbye to a sole traveler. Half of our class had come to bid farewell to Fatima, even the ones who never talked to us. They were standing around her in a circle, giving out phone numbers, asking to stay in touch. "Don't forget your friends back here," I overheard someone say, followed by a laugh that sounded like a horse neighing. Fatima was the first one of our group to leave. I observed from the side. The sense of loss I was feeling was overwhelming. I was losing my closest friend, my confidant, my sister-in-mischief. I knew that we were only being separated by distance, that we would keep in touch on the phone until we saw each other again, yet I knew that something was irreparably breaking. I knew deep down that we would never again be as close as the way we were right then. Our lives were going in different directions, and we were bound to grow apart. She would move on with her new life in a new country, attend a new school, make new friends, and maybe have a boyfriend and then a husband and children one day. I would move on with mine, although I was not sure exactly where it was headed at that point. Our chats would be long and thrilling in the beginning, but they would become shorter with time, then there would be long laps of silence, with an occasional rushed catch-up call in between; then maybe one day, there would be nothing. I would be the girl she had gone to school with back home, her long-lost childhood friend.

I felt a hand on my shoulder. I looked back, and it was Fatima's father. He did not say a word, but his eyes and his knowing smile said that even though the situation looked dire, everything would be okay. Fatima's mom was standing next to him with a handkerchief in her hands, and occasionally she dabbed her red eyes. She was feeling the apprehension of imminent separation as well; her only daughter was going away to a foreign land. She was probably consoled by the fact that one day Fatima would come back with a head full of knowledge and shiny university diplomas that she would proudly hang in her living room. I looked at Fatima working herself out of the circle she was trapped in and walking toward me. After much back and forth, we had decided that she would travel simple, therefore dress simple. We chose for her a pair of blue jeans, a yellow top with fringes on the sleeves, and black Adidas sneakers. We packed a sweater that we had struggled to find in the Madina market in her backpack, in case she got cold. She had gotten her hair braided the day before, and the long braids fell freely on her back. She had put on some eye shadow and pinkish lipstick. She was happy, her face was lit up, and her eyes were sparkly. I took a mental picture of her. When it was time to go, we hugged. We stayed silent in the middle of the commotion around us. We stayed silent because we each knew what the other was thinking. We stayed silent because even though we had a million words to say, they just couldn't convey what we were feeling. We stayed silent because words would just be superfluous.

I went back to my life. My life in my new home. The numbness of separation gradually faded away. Life in my new home was an adjustment, but tuning in to a new situation was no longer foreign to me. Bouba had been the buffer while he was there, creating a neutral zone between his mother and I. Bouba's mother asked me to move into the big house the day he left, but I told her I preferred staying in the small guesthouse. She looked at me for a long moment, a long, dragged-out stare down. I looked away and continued peeling the eggplant in my hand, focusing on how purple it was. I overheard her complaining to Bouba that evening when I was sitting in the prayer gazebo. Her voice carried through the living room window, which was open. He did not mention it when he called me. We were on slightly better terms since the day I had received the exam results. The relationship with my mother-in-law was tense for a few days, but it eventually returned to some type of normalcy.

Every day, the whole household woke up before sunrise at the muezzin's call and congregated under the prayer gazebo for the dawn prayer. Bouba's father led the prayer. He was a tall, dark, sturdy man of very few words. After prayer, he remained on his mat, reflexively going through his prayer beads while the rest of the household buzzed around, going about the morning tasks. I prepared breakfast every morning. Fried eggs, sometimes corned beef with bread, some mboiri, or fouti at other times. I set up the foldable table on the patio, then neatly arranged the food on it. I carefully filled the thermos with hot kinkeliba tea, then put it next to the pack of St. Louis Sugar and Gloria milk. I always completed a last check: main dish, bread, thermos, butter, sugar, milk, plates, flatware, mugs. I did not want to leave the door open for any reprimand. After I was done, Bouba's parents would sit at the table. My mother-in-law would chat away while cutting a piece of bread, buttering it, and putting it on her husband's plate, who remained silent while eating. Once done with breakfast, she would bring him his bag and walk him to the car. Mamadou would vigorously wipe the car a few more times in an overdone manner before opening the door for him. He left us to our daily activities. My mother-in-law sat in the living room to await her daily visitors, Mamadou swept the courtyard, and I went to the market. When he came home in the evenings, he sat on the patio with a book or paper in his hands until dinner was served. After dinner, he sometimes watched the news on TV while sitting in his rocking chair, and other times he would head straight back upstairs until the next morning at prayer time.

That was my new life. Wake up. Prayer. Kitchen. Breakfast. Market. Kitchen. Lunch. Rest. Clean my small apartment. Kitchen. Dinner. Prayer. Bouba's call. TV. Bedtime. Bouba's sisters barely came down from their rooms, let alone entered the kitchen; sometimes I could hear their loud laughs from the courtyard. They spent most of their time doing their hair, trying on makeup, and going to the high school basketball court in the late afternoons to hang out with their friends. I wished for an invitation even though I was older than them and their group of friends, but it never came. Fatima's calls were the highlights of my weeks. She often called on Saturdays. She was living with her uncle and his wife. Life was not as she had imagined, and she would not be living on campus as she had thought. She missed home and found the food there bland. She was constantly cold, and she could not get used to all the snow on the ground. There was so much snow that she struggled to walk to her bus stop some mornings. I looked forward to listening to her complaints; it was an evasion from my daily life. I wished I had her problems.

Aunty visited twice. She sat in the living room with my mother-in-law for almost an hour before coming to the guesthouse. I gave her a quick tour, and we sat in the bedroom for a short while. She inquired about my life and asked whether I was treating my in-laws with respect. I had to remember that I was representing our entire family in that house. She came with Ousbi the second time, and he stayed with me for a couple of days, sleeping on the small sofa in the living room. He had grown up so suddenly. At fourteen, he was almost as tall me. His facial features were becoming more defined, and his voice was getting deeper. We talked about his classes, how life was back at the house with Aunty and Uncle. Koto had promised to get him a phone like the one I had. I stared at him when he was not looking. My baby brother was turning into a young man. I went back to Kissosso some Sundays. It was odd—the house where I had spent the last ten years of my life was different. It felt familiar, yet I also felt out of place. Batouly was still humming her tunes while going about her work. When I opened the armoire in the bedroom, it had been rearranged. Batouly's stuff filled my side of it now. I no longer had a place in the house. Life went on.

Ramadan came , bringing with it its austere mood, daunting long days, and pungent breaths. When Neneh was alive, Ramadan had been an event we looked forward to. We spent the days leading up to it squinting our little eyes at the sky at sundown, looking for the moon, the faint crescent that barely glinted, marking the start of the holy month. We had competitions with the neighbor's children about who could last the longest without sneaking in a drink or a snack when no one was looking. We looked forward to foutouro, sitting up on the roof or at the edge of the fence, waiting for the call to prayer of the muezzin at sunset, signaling the end of the fasting day. It was exhilarating watching the adults rush for the food after prayer and waiting around the adults' table to pick out the delicious foods that had not made it to the kids' table. We looked forward to the long special evening prayers after dinner, the rush of waking up before sunup to stuff our tiny faces with food and drinks, and the sleepover at the mosque for Laylatul Qadr; but most important, for us children, the month was less about the spiritual components and more about planning, picking, and making that Eid outfit that would be the best of the neighborhood.

One thing that I never liked about Ramadan was the constant spitting, as well as watching people eat the traditional tori meal. It consisted of cassava flour that was cooked in boiling water and pounded in a laborious way with a sturdy wooden stick with a wide V at its bottom until the mixture was smooth. The mixture was scooped from the pot with a ladle, which gave it a rounded shape, and it made a *plop* sound when dropped into the nama sauce, a stew made with grounded okra and smoked fish. The sauce was green, and Koto would not partake in it, always wondering why people would eat that dish, and on top of that, eat it in a collective bowl. My stomach felt queasy as a memory of the gate man Mamadou licking the slimy gumbo sauce as it trickled down his forearm came to my mind.

As a new housewife, Ramadan was more about keeping up with my duties of being in the kitchen, cooking up elaborate meals for my in-laws and a house full of hungry people, cleaning up after the meals at sundown, and preparing the sougouli meals for the next day, all while fasting, spiritually meditating, and cultivating my relationship with God—the same as the men who were always lazily sprawled out on mats or hammocks and slumbering under the trees. The imam had addressed men at the first Ramadan prayer, urging them to help the women with the chores so that they, too, could partake in the month's blessings to the fullest, but all the assistance I got was when they diligently emptied their platefuls of food and set them right back on the table to be picked up by me. The men never helped on ordinary days; why would they help now? Why preach for men to help with the house chores only during Ramadan; how about preaching about it year-round? I never understood it. Men were supposed to be the strength, the backbone of the household, yet they got away with doing the least possible. I spent so much time in that kitchen that I felt like one of its props. The pots, the pans, the mortar, the charcoal stove, the calabash, the stool, the broom, the bag of charcoal, and Amina. I just wanted it to be over with. I wanted my visa to be approved. What if my visa was denied? Would this be my life from now on? I pushed the thought away. I wanted to go to the US. I wanted to go to university. I wanted to be closer to Fatima. This life I was living was not mine. It did not feel like the life I was supposed to live.

Chapter Ten

After seven long months, it finally arrived. Bouba forwarded me the email. I stared at the message for several minutes and reread the words on the screen.

We are pleased to inform you that we have scheduled your immigrant visa interview on February 13, 2006, at the U.S. Embassy or Consulate in CONAKRY, GUINEA. This interview is for immigrant visa case filed by BOUBACAR BARRY on behalf of AMINATOU BARRY.

It was followed by more details, a couple of pages of instructions, a full-page list of original documents to bring to the appointment, and instructions on a medical examination to complete by an embassy-approved physician prior to the interview. I had exactly forty-six days to prepare. I felt overwhelmed, but at last something was happening. I had started having nightmares about being stuck like the women whose husbands had gone to sea for years, leaving their wives to fend for themselves; about living from handouts from Bouba and his parents; about being a docile and obedient housewife to my in-laws; about being a docile, obedient, celibate wife. I instinctively wanted to call Fatima, but I realized it was not yet morning in Montreal. I printed the documents, paid the girl at the cybercafe counter, and walked out onto the busy sidewalk. I walked instead of grabbing a taxi. I was lost in my reverie. There was renewed hope. That night, I dreamt of tall buildings, fancy malls, big trucks, and bustling streets.

The forty-six days went by slow as a snail. I busied myself with mindless tasks. I rearranged my folder of papers over a thousand times, making sure I had an original and copies and English translations. I completed my medical exam and X-rays at Clinique Pasteur. I had been perplexed by one of the questions during the medical exam: "Do you have a communicable disease of public health significance?" The physician gave examples when he saw my puzzled face. "Tuberculosis? HIV? Syphilis? Here is a list. We are going to conduct some tests, but you should know that having a communicable disease of public health significance would make an alien inadmissible in the US." I stared at him, then at the paper he handed to me. Still boggled after my exam, I made a detour to the cybercafe to see if I could get some answers. I typed in the search bar: *Communicable Diseases USA Immigration.* I scrolled through the results. I remembered Bouba telling me to pay attention to the links and sources of the information I read on the internet. A ".gov" extension is credible, I thought, clicking on it. I found out that the medical reasons barring entrance to the United States included mental health disorders, substance abuse, epilepsy, tuberculosis, leprosy, syphilis, gonorrhea, or "any dangerous contagious disease." The discovery of HIV and the economic and political climate of the 1980s had led to its addition on the list. The large incursion of immigrants in the 1980s and the economic recession sparked concerns about immigrants taking American jobs and being a burden on the American health and welfare systems, so President Reagan had required all immigrants to be tested for these diseases, making infected aliens effectively ineligible for admission. I wondered how many people were denied access for these reasons, some of them probably unaware of their conditions, or others hoping to leave to have access to care. I wondered if the Guinean authorities asked Americans if they had a "communicable disease of public significance" when they wanted to come to Guinea.

I thought I was early when I went to my visa appointment, but there was already a long, winding queue in front of the consulate window. I speculated on how many people would be denied visas that day for various reasons. I was dizzy throughout the whole process—when the man at the window checked my appointment letter; when I passed through the security line; when people were called to the windows one by one; when the older woman before me who intended to visit her son who had just become a father was denied; when my name was called and I sat in front of the officer, my hands damp and my voice shaky, while she scrutinized my papers and asked me questions that had already been answered on the visa form. I felt dizzier when she remained silent for what seemed like an eternity, energetically striking the keys on her keyboard, then she handed me a paper. Her voice was detached. "You can collect your passport in two days at the pick-up window. Congratulations." After months of preparations, weeks of fretting, and nearly two hours of waiting in that room, the interview had barely taken five minutes. I do not remember how I made my way out of the embassy. The ground was soft and fluffy, the air sweet, and the guards in uniforms seemed much friendlier. At last, I also had that valuable piece of paper affixed to my passport, effectively changing the course of my life. I flashed a big smile at Mamady in the distance as he waited for me in the parking lot, sitting on the hood of his dad's car.

I counted it. Sixty-three lighted fires. Sixty-three cooked and served dinners. Sixty-three nights spent in the small bedroom in the back of the house between the day I had obtained my visa and my upcoming departure date. Bouba purchased my ticket four weeks after my visa was approved and instructed me to pick it up at Royal Air Maroc agency downtown. I had read the French version of the welcome-to-America packet I had received at the embassy from front to back. Welcome to the United States: A Guide for New Immigrants. I started reading my old English notebooks, trying to memorize phrases and imagining myself in settings where I would use them. I went to visit Aunty, Uncle, and Ousbi to say my goodbyes. I knew they would be at the airport, but I wanted to say goodbye properly. Ousbi hugged me and cried shy tears as we stood in the back of the house, looking in the distance at Mount Kakoulima. I promised him I would do whatever it takes to bring him to the US as soon as I was in a position to do so. I made him promise me to stay out of trouble and to keep up with school. I gave him my phone so that Koto and I could call him directly. His face lit up and he jumped in joy, taking off soon after to go show off his new phone to his friends, his lanky body bobbing up and down the road. Aunty gave me more advice—I felt that all our interactions now started and ended with advice. "Have your children as soon as you can so you can get it out of the way. And have them close in age; it will be hard at first, but you will see, it will be much better for you." I nodded, although that was not something I had given any thought to or intended to do; besides, at the rate it had started, intimacy with Bouba would certainly be a challenge. She gave me the phone number of her cousin who lived in Virginia, directing me to call and visit her when I arrived. I visited Ms. Tawel, who told me to hold off on having children and to focus on getting enrolled in college. Uncle was out of town, so we called him, and I listened quietly as he wheedled me to carry on as I had been so far and to make the family proud. Koto promised to travel from Rabat to the Casablanca airport to see me during my layover.

My sendoffs with my husband's family were hasty, awkward, and devoid of genuineness. Our relationship had never warmed up, and I was relieved to be leaving my in-laws' house at last. "We're coming soon, too, as soon as we're done with high school," Bouba's sisters said almost in unison. I cleaned the guesthouse from top to bottom, made the bed, scoured the place for any remaining belongings, and gave half of my clothes to Oumi and Batouly. My luggage was filled with dried catfish, shrimp powder, palm oil, and meticulously wrapped cassava leaves. "Make sure you put these in the freezer as soon as you arrive, and they will last you for months. My Bouba does love his cassava leaves," my mother-in-law said as she shoved the remaining bags in the suitcase. The news traveled fast because, once again, our entire class was at the airport, going through the same routine as with Fatima, even though my flight was scheduled at 1 a.m. I understood how Fatima felt that day. I was sad to leave my family and friends behind, but I was ecstatic about the new adventure that lay ahead of me. I had carefully picked out a pink polo shirt, faded black jeans, and new black canvas sneakers to wear for my journey. I imagined that was how an eighteen-year-old American woman would dress to travel, and I wanted to blend in as much as possible. I brushed my tight curls into a high bun and applied a light coat of a pale, natural-colored lipstick that had been included in my wedding gifts but that I never wore. A brand-new life. Anxiety grabbed at me until I boarded the plane, only half believing that I was actually leaving, expecting someone to stop me at security, or at customs, or again at the preboarding check. I only relaxed when the aircraft picked up speed on the runway, taking off into the cool air of the night, carrying me to a new chapter in my life.

We arrived in Casablanca, Morocco, at six in the morning. The air was significantly cooler than in Conakry when we stepped off the plane to board a bus that would take us to the main terminal. Koto had told me to follow the travelers who were exiting the airport so he could meet me beyond the checkpoints. I trailed the sea of boubous, caftans, and turbans across the halls. Morocco was a visa-free country for Guineans, so tourists who couldn't travel to Europe or the US, as well as students, merchants, and ill people in search of better hospitals, all flocked to the country despite the fact that the red carpet was not exactly rolled out for them. The officer behind the window at the police checkpoint barely looked up while inspecting my passport and asked me what the purpose of my trip was. I explained that I would be boarding another flight in three hours and was only entering the territory for a quick visit. He flipped through the pages of my passport before stamping it and unceremoniously throwing it back at me. How rude, I thought to myself, walking away and following the exit signs. I heard Koto's voice before I saw him. "Amina!" I looked in the direction where the voice had come from, and I was overcome with joy when I saw him running toward me. Tears trickled down my cheeks. Tears of happiness. We stood hugging each other while other travelers moved around us, then walked hand in hand to the café right outside.

"Oh my god! How you have changed!" he exclaimed.

"And how you have gotten fat!!" I teased him back. He was definitely rounder than when he had left Conakry. Seated there, looking at him, punching him in his shoulder, talking, and laughing together felt unreal. It felt like the old times when we sat on the roof of our house in Simbayah, talking about our dreams. I would have never imagined that this was how we would see each other again, in an airport, counting the minutes until we had to part, but I gladly took it. I filled him in on what had been happening back home, and he told me about his job, his life, and how Uncle had started calling him to remind him that it was time to go home and find a wife. He told me that he had no intention of doing so, that he would marry when he met the one for him, and that there was no shortage of eligible young women around the university town. Time flew. Elation was replaced with the sadness of parting ways again, but this time around, it was less painful as I was feeling more hopeful about the future. Koto asked me to send him my new phone number as soon as I obtained one before he waved goodbye as I walked back toward the police checkpoints.

After eight and a half interminable hours, I arrived in Washington Dulles airport in the afternoon. I was shocked by the stark difference in the plane that had taken me from Conakry to Morocco compared to the one that we traveled on to Washington. The first plane was rundown, smelled like urine toward the back, and the fabric on some of the seats was ripped. The second aircraft in contrast was comfy, clean, and odorless; and the seats had blankets and small pillows on them. Even the flight attendants were nicer. I looked through the window as the airplane slowly pulled up to the deplaning area, and the sun was extremely bright. The man sitting next to me removed his dress shoes and replaced them with traditionally sewn leather sandals, the kind I saw men wearing in the village. They were made of dried cow skin that had been left in the sun to dry for days, but they still carried a smell. I caught a whiff of the shoes and wrinkled my nose. I found his action bizarre, especially since it was still March in Washington, DC, and everyone else was bundling up.

Elation enveloped me as I tailed the other travelers exiting the plane, but soon I found myself in an enormous queue at passport control. There were people from all over the world, speaking various languages. I entered the line for permanent residents, as my booklet had instructed me to, and slowly inched my way through, clutching my passport like a treasure. When the man in uniform waved at me to advance, I walked to his booth and handed him my passport. He swiped it into his computer system, and without a word, he flipped through the pages until he found the visa stamp. I had heard of people being searched, interrogated, and even sent back at immigration. I said a little prayer in my head. He asked me a few questions, and I wished I had paid more attention in English class. He then requested the X-ray from my medical exam and my sealed immigration packet. It must have taken only a few seconds, though it seemed like an eternity; but finally, he stamped my passport, handed it back to me, and nonchalantly said, "Welcome to the United States." I grabbed my passport, smiled, and calmly walked away; but in my head, I was doing cartwheels. I was in the United States of America. I had a sudden urge to pee.

I tried to get a cart for my luggage like the other travelers, but after a labored exchange in hand signs and the little

English I knew with an airport worker, I found out that it cost five dollars. I did a little calculation in my head and figured that it would amount to almost forty thousand Guinean francs. I will lug this luggage myself, I thought as I gathered my bags and started rolling my two suitcases toward the arrival area. There were dogs sniffing people's luggage, and the customs signs warned that bringing in fruits and some other food products was not allowed. I remembered the dried fish, palm oil, and cassava leaves in my bags. In my rush, I had not checked the detailed list. I was worried that one of the dogs would detect them and that they would pull me aside and send me back on the next flight. No such thing happened.

Bouba was waving at me in the arrival area. For a moment, I forgot the circumstances in which I had found myself there; I forgot all my anger toward him and ran to hug him. He smelled of fresh, breezy laundry. He helped me roll the suitcases. The bright, shining sun pulled a fast one on me, because I felt the cold bite me as soon as we stepped beyond the sliding doors. "Welcome to America!" he said joyfully as he saw me shiver under the jacket he had given me. The short walk to the car felt like a kilometer. He turned the car on and asked me to sit inside while he loaded the bags. I felt relief when he slammed the trunk of the car closed because the cold air was getting in.

"Is this your car?" I asked him as he slid into the driver seat.

"Yes. Can't survive without a car here!" he said, then added, "Put your seat belt on. You are not in Guinea anymore." He smiled.

The car was clean and smelled like fresh trees. It was a gray Toyota. I had read the word *Camry* out loud when we approached the car. it. As we drove off, I excitedly told him about my trip, about reuniting with Koto in Casablanca, about the state of the first plane I had traveled in. When I mentioned the man with the sandals, he burst out laughing before saying, "He probably had some talisman sewn into those shoes so that he wouldn't be turned away at immigration."

"Too bad I lost track of him, so we will never know if it worked!" I laughed as we cruised down the highway. I felt light and alive.

Chapter Eleven

America surprised me. The highway from the airport was imposing, a far cry from the four unmarked lanes we called a highway back home. I, however, expected to see skyscrapers and shining signs everywhere like in the movies, but all I saw was a succession of strip malls and housing units. I was shocked by the flags. There were flags everywhere. Flying on poles on the side of the roads, in front yards, on the sides of cars. The only place I saw a flag at home was at the People's Palace downtown, or in the schoolyard during school hours. Bouba explained to me that Americans may squabble about politics and policies, but they were patriotic at the core, and even more so since the 9/11 attacks that happened almost five years ago. There was no honking, and all the cars drove in civility next to each other, following the rules of the road. Everything was clean and tidy. All the streets had names, and all the buildings were numbered. There was no ambiguity in addresses, such as turning right at the big flamboyant tree, passing the garage at the top of the hill, then making a left at the corner where the mango vendor sits. Cars stopped at lights to let pedestrians cross the streets, and the lights flashed to let people know how much time they had left before the light turned. I also noticed that houses were not secured by high fences; bikes, toys, and furniture were scattered freely across the yards, and cars were parked in driveways without anyone watching. America surprised me.

The sun was setting by the time we arrived at Bouba's apartment in Hyattsville, Maryland. I was physically exhausted, having been awake for almost twenty-four hours. I looked up at the massive building when we got out of the car and started moving from one foot to the other as he unloaded the suitcases, feeling the cold bite my face again.

"We are on the ninth floor," Bouba shouted from the back of the car. "You can start walking; I bet you are cold. I will meet you by the elevators at the entrance." He pointing toward the building. I welcomed the warmer temperature when we walked into the apartment. It looked plain and barely lived in. The living area, dining space, and kitchen were all connected in one room. There was a small table with two chairs pushed against the half wall that separated the kitchen and the dining room. The sofa was brown, almost matching the color of the coffee table. The gigantic TV was the centerpiece of the room, taking up almost all of the space on the stand on which it stood. The walls were bare, and there were no curtains, just blinds hanging over a large door that led to a balcony. There was only one lock on the door. Down the hall, I saw a light glare from a room that I assumed to be the bedroom where I could hear Bouba dropping my bags. I walked to the kitchen and stood in the middle, looking around for a minute. I turned the kitchen faucet on and water came rushing out, splashing all around the sink and my polo shirt I quickly turned it off. Bouba had walked up just then, and he looked at me, smiling, before he said, "Yes, hot water twenty-four seven. Power twenty-four seven. And the water pressure is great; you'll see." I opened the top door of the large white fridge and a cold burst of air rushed out of it. It was empty except for a couple of food containers. It had so much space, and it didn't have the smell of the freezer back home—the smell of food that never fully freezes and keeps unthawing and refreezing on a loop because of the power cuts.

"There is no food, so I am going to order us a pizza. We will buy groceries tomorrow. I took the day off." There was a moment of silence before he said, "Well, make yourself at home. This is your home. And don't just stand there; come, let me show you where the bathroom is and where you can put your clothes." I followed him down the hall. The bedroom was twice the size of the one we had back home but was very modest, like the rest of the apartment—a bed and two nightstands with lamps. You could walk into the wardrobe—"a walk-in closet," Bouba called it. "All this room for clothes? Someone could sleep in here," I remarked to him. It was odd that he had only a few shirts hanging in that large walk-in closet. I thought about how I would arrange my clothes, and just then remembered the food in my luggage.

"Oh, I have food to put in the freezer before it spoils."

"Sure, if you can get it out of the suitcase. I will take care of it while you shower and change."

The smell of dried fish enveloped the bedroom as soon as I opened the bag. Bouba cracked the window open and took the food to the kitchen. Thankfully, my clothes were in the other bag, or I would have been walking around smelling like smoked catfish. The shower was heavenly.

I was in awe of the oversized pizza and the equally hefty bottle of Coke. I grabbed a slice that was heavy with meat and cheese. It tasted odd in my mouth; I had never had that combination of bread, tomato, cheese, and meat. We enjoyed the evening watching TV from the dining table, scarcely talking as we ate and watched a show called *60 Minutes.* I was now like the little kids back home who followed the images and tried to construe what was happening on the screen. I asked Bouba if they were speaking English. The American accent sounded strange to me, completely different from the one I was used to hearing on the BBC. We sat there until I couldn't keep my eyes open any longer. When I laid in bed, I tried to replay all the moments of the previous hours like a video in rewind. I still couldn't believe where I was. My first day in America had been good, I thought as I drifted off to sleep.

The next morning, Bouba took me to Walmart to pick up some sweaters, winter shoes, a new phone, and groceries. My African eyes were awestruck by what they saw. I had never seen a store where you could buy groceries, clothes, electronics, a tire for your car, and prescription medicine in one shop. The sheer size of the place was shocking. I was starting to get it: everything in America was twice the size or more than the regular—the roads, the cars, the houses, the apartments, the food portions, and even the people. I pushed the double-sized shopping cart through rows of laundry detergents, coffee machines, jewelry, toiletries, and toys before we arrived at the food section. There, too, the memo had been received about size. I palmed a massive eggplant, trying to figure out how many regular-sized eggplants I could cut it into. We bought groceries for days and filled the cart to the brim since, apparently, people in America did not buy fresh produce from the market every day. I discovered that you could buy virtually everything premade in the frozen section: breakfast, pizza, dinner trays, chicken. There were hundreds of options to choose from for a single item. I had thought bread was just bread, but there was white bread, wheat bread, potato bread, rye bread, pumpernickel bread, sourdough bread, sweet Hawaiian bread...the varieties were endless. And I did not know there were so many variations of milk—whole milk, reduced-fat two percent, one percent, skim, soy milk, almond milk, and so on. Then, once you were settled on which type you wanted, you could move on to choosing a brand. Repeat in each aisle. How much choice did one person need? I involuntarily heard a voice ask in my head. What amazed me even more was that the store trusted customers to weigh and label items by themselves. I thought about how that would work back home; there wouldn't be a store before long.

Bouba bought me a new phone with a prepaid plan, a clear upgrade from the one I had previously had. It was called a smartphone. Its screen lit up with a dozen icons, and I could browse the internet, listen to music, and even send and receive email on it. I was delighted. When it was time to pay, however, there was another surprise. The price on the tag was not the one you paid; a sales tax was added. The day was a succession of surprises. I called everyone as soon as we got back home with an international calling card we had bought on the way back. Fatima first, Koto next, then Ousbi, who passed the phone to Aunty and Uncle, who was back. I started telling them about my adventures after long minutes of greeting, but the call was interrupted because all the minutes on the calling card had been used up. I called Aunty's cousin in Virginia, and she invited us to come over to her house one weekend but to make sure to call first and confirm that she was not working.

The disenchantment was not slow to arrive. I was in a foreign country with a person I barely knew, living in a small one-bedroom apartment in Hyattsville, Maryland. I was alone most of the time as Bouba was constantly working. I felt trapped in the apartment. We couldn't start any procedures since I had to wait for my green card, which was set to arrive within three months from my entry into American territory. I needed a social security number to obtain just about everything, from an identification card to a bank account, or if I wanted to seek employment. I compulsively checked the mailbox every day even though I knew it was too early, but I was hoping that somehow it would arrive earlier than planned because someone, somewhere, was really diligent about their job, which solely consisted of putting green cards in envelopes and mailing them out. We lived in a high-rise where it seemed every other resident was either from Haiti, Mexico, Vietnam, Nigeria, or Pakistan. I sometimes wandered in the building, imagining who lived behind the door with the loud TV, or the one with the barking dog, or again the one with the screaming children. The hallways were always filled with a mixture of smells, spices, and aromas from cooking stews, fried fish, and incense. I would know that someone had just come out of the building by catching a whiff of that scent in the parking lot. I spent lonely days watching daytime TV, focusing on the closed captioning, trying to pick up new words and pronunciations, understand the accent, and learn how to put sentences together. I watched the *Today Show*, the news, the *Oprah Winfrey Show*, *Judge Judy*, the *Ellen DeGeneres Show*, *Sesame Street*, *106 & Park*, reruns of *Moesha*, *Girlfriends*.... I watched everything, and when I was in the kitchen, I listened in the background.

I busied myself rearranging the little furniture there was in the apartment, cleaning and cooking, and attempting to take walks around the neighborhood, but I soon realized that beyond the apartment complex, the area was not very walkable. The streets were geared for moving vehicles, not for pedestrians. I sometimes gazed out from our ninth-floor windows, looking at life happening outside, eager to be one of the people going to school, work, or wherever they were headed. I browsed the internet and emailed back and forth with Fatima several times a day. The internet speed was absurdly fast. I studied the Maryland Driver's Manual and memorized signs. I completed the same routine every day and fidgeted around the apartment like a mad person when I ran out of things to do. I asked Bouba to teach me how to use the bus and metro system one weekend, and my life changed.

A new world opened up to me. I hurriedly cooked and cleaned every morning before leaving the apartment and catching the bus. I spent my afternoons on a different bus line every day, from one end to the terminus and back. I preferred the bus because, unlike the metro, I could look through the large windows and discover this new country. At first sight, one might think that all Americans do is eat and shop. Shops and restaurants everywhere. They were lined up on stretches of miles. McDonald's, Wendy's, TJMaxx. Burger King, Taco Bell, Marshalls. Popeyes, Red Robin, Ross. Olive Garden. A mall. Red Lobster, Burlington Coat Factory. Over and over again. When I went inside the mall, different types of stores and shopping were revealed to me, but it was still the same. Floors of stores, and a food court for when you wanted to replenish your energy. Eat and shop. It was a relief when we went to visit Washington, DC, the National Mall, and the Smithsonian museums. I was thrilled to see a different side of the metropolitan area; for a short while there, I had thought America was all strip malls and shopping malls.

I was becoming more confident in my interactions. Americans liked to talk. It always started with "Where are you from?" or "Where is that accent from?" I chatted with people on the bus, sometimes using my phone to look up words. I started getting off the bus to explore. I chatted with people in shops. I tried new foods. I learned new things, such as the fact that there was a line for everything—the grocery store, the coffee shop, the cinema, the restrooms. Americans said "O" instead of zero. I was confused when a hairdresser gave me her contact one day and started her phone number with "three-O-one." *Gas* meant fuel, a *cup of joe* meant coffee, *soda* meant a soft drink, a *John Hancock* meant a signature, *cop* meant a police officer, the term *ride* could be used to refer to a car, and other bizarre references. The money was not just notes but also coins, and a *bill* was a note. Imperial units of measurements were used instead of the metric system. I was confused by square feet, gallons, miles, and pounds. Temperatures were in Fahrenheit instead of Celsius. I could not understand how the weather forecast on the news said it would be thirty degrees when it was freezing outside. I learned that church and sports were the cornerstones of the community; that pharmacies sold food and cigarettes and developed photos; that comedians could make fun of the president on TV without fear of repercussions; that there was a sale for every holiday; and that the dog slept in the house. I also learned that there were Black neighborhoods, white neighborhoods, and Hispanic and Asian neighborhoods; that if you are half Black, then you are Black; that Hispanic people are considered Mexicans, that many Americans thought Africa was a country where people lived with the animals in the jungle; that Americans love Taco Tuesdays and Cinco de Mayo, but they didn't like Mexicans because they were taking their jobs; and that Islam equals terrorism and other negative generalizations, but I took it all in, sorted it out to the best I could, and sought to learn more. I came home with my head buzzing, turned the TV on, and started reheating dinner. My cooking time had been exponentially reduced and become much simpler. What once took me the better part of the day back home only took me an hour at most. It took a second to ignite the gas fire and put the meat in the pan; minutes to blend condiments in the mixer, concoct sauces, and let them simmer while I worked the vacuum cleaner; and when I came home from my adventures, all I had to do was put the food in the microwave to reheat. What a wonderful appliance that microwave was.

Bouba and I were back to square one. We lived like a couple of friends who happened to share a bed. He came home late, showered, ate the dinner I had set on the table, and watched the *Daily Show with Jon Stewart* before heading to bed. He was usually fast asleep by the time I came into the bedroom. He was not mired by complexity; there was something almost abnormal about his simplicity. He methodically did the same things every day, in the same order, and it irked me. He was diligent about making sure I had everything I needed, but he spoke very little, just like his father. It was impossible to read him or know what was going on behind his forehead; it was as if I were living with a male version of Batouly, only I was married to him. We went out to the movies together, ate dinner together, and shared things, but when night came, he turned the other way. I didn't know why he didn't touch me, but I couldn't help but think the reason was me somehow. Was it maybe because he didn't believe I had been a virgin that night? I wasn't even sure I actually wanted him to touch me. I recoiled at the memory of his last night in Conakry, and how his touch had felt rough and his manhood unpleasant. I secretly wished that he would never touch me again, but it must have been some type of conceit, or maybe insecurity, to need to feel desired by the stranger laying in bed next to me. I tossed and turned, wondered, and asked questions in my head that I could not push out of my mouth. Sometimes I cried, but it was in short spurts. I remembered that there was a whole world out there for me to explore. When I left the apartment, I was a different person. It was as if a weight was lifted off me, a layer of skin removed. I felt new, alive. I saw the world around me clearer and brighter, and I felt every new experience intensely.

My green card finally arrived. I promptly applied and interviewed for a social security number, which I found out I could have actually started the process for with just my visa, but that water had already spilt anyway. The card was mailed to me within two weeks. The next step in the *Amina Gets Settled in America* book was to obtain an American identification card. Saying that the trip to the Motor Vehicle Administration was trying is an understatement. Bouba took a half day off in anticipation because going to the MVA was never a quick in-and-out mission, he said. We took a number at 1:40 p.m. and took a seat. Around us, there were people from all corners of the world—male, female, young, and old. The last time I had seen such a concentration of diversity was at the airport on the day I arrived. Sitting in front of me was a young mother who looked through her phone while her child kept climbing and jumping on the chair next to her. The man next to me was visibly stressed as he tapped his leg restlessly, flicking his lighter open and close incessantly. I opened my manual and started reviewing it one last time, but I was unable to concentrate on the words in front of me. An hour passed. The little child in front of us started crying and throwing himself on the floor while his mother looked on indifferently. Someone at the window was screaming that he had to get back to work and couldn't possibly leave to pick up a document and get back in line. I tried tuning out my surroundings, but the person behind me was talking loudly on the phone in a language I did not understand. My head buzzed. Our number was called at 4:25 p.m., and we were told that it was too late for me to take my knowledge test. "Come back tomorrow!" the woman rudely said before getting up and walking away from her workstation. I was frustrated because I had mentally prepared myself for the test and waited more than two hours just to be turned away. Bouba had to work the next day, so we agreed that he would drop me off on his way to work the next day after I assured him that I could manage alone.

I arrived before the doors opened the next day and took a spot in the already-winding line. I took a number at 9:10 a.m. and took a seat. The room was filling up pretty fast. Bouba had ranted for a good part of the previous evening. Going to the MVA was tantamount to frustration. The best way to reasonably have freedom of movement in America is to have a car, but if you need to drive, then you need the MVA; if you want to buy a new car, then you need the MVA to register, so you had to contend with the long lines, rude employees, and bureaucracy because there was no way around it. To think I could just buy a license back home, I told him. "Well, that is actually a whole different problem!" he said, laughing it off. My number was called at 11:20 a.m. I rushed to the window.

"Good morning," I hesitantly said to the woman.

"How can I help you?" she responded, barely looking up from her computer. I pushed my documents toward her and said slowly, measuring each word, "I need a learner's permit." She looked up and brashly replied, "You need a what now?" I took a breath and repeated myself, enunciating better. She squinted her eyes for a second before calling out, "Tammy, can you come over here for a minute; I cannot understand what she is saying." I pulled the application we had filled out the prior day out of the pile and tapped on it.

141

"Oh, a learner's permit! Never mind, Tammy." I guess my accent was incomprehensible. She looked through my documents, green card, social security card, and notarized affidavit from Bouba for proof of address. She flipped through as if she was looking for more.

"Your file is not complete. You need two proofs of address." I blinked at her, not understanding. She pointed at the document and repeated herself, looking exasperated.

"Your file is not complete. You need two proofs of address." She sighed when I kept looking at her and continued speaking slowly. I understood what she had said; did she think that repeating the exact same words in slow motion would help? "I need another document with your name and address on it. Electric bill? Water bill? Bank statement?" I remembered that I had the mailing envelope and letter that my social security card had come in inside my folder. I set my purse on the counter and pulled the folder out, looking for the piece of paper, praying to god that I indeed had it, and praying that I wouldn't have to leave and come back a third day because of a tiny piece of paper. I found it and handed it to her, half relieved and half expecting her to ask for something else. She put all the documents through a scanner, then told me to step up to the machine for my vision test. I peeped into the binocular-looking machine and lifted my face, asking the woman which line I should read, holding up my fingers to count. I read the letters on the first line loud and clear, making sure not to confuse my French and English alphabet. She then escorted me to the testing room and instructed me to sit at a computer and start the test whenever I was ready. I exhaled a big sigh of relief when I passed. At least I did not have to come back and start this process all over again.

I was hungry and thirsty when I was sent back to the big hall for even more waiting. A quick glance around revealed that there were no vending machines in the waiting room, and I was terrified of leaving even for a couple of minutes to buy water at the risk of missing my name being called. It was odd, given the constant presence of snack vending machines in every other waiting room I had been to before. After what seemed like an eternity, I heard someone call my name. I was not sure at first as it was a distorted version of "Aminatou," but after two calls I recognized it as their attempt at pronouncing my name, so I stood up and hurried to the window. I paid the fee, waited a little longer, and finally, at 2:20 p.m., I walked out of the building brandishing my brand-new ticket to the roads of America.

Chapter Twelve

We visited Aunty Hassanatou's cousin the following weekend. She had taken time off from her second job so she could receive us. Bouba seemed tense during the drive. I mainly looked out the window, and we barely talked. The room was more than ever quiet, the air stiller when we were in the presence of each other. We were both set in our routines and spent one hour at most together during dinner before we both went back to our own activities. When I called Aunty weekly, I told her everything was fine whenever she inquired. I kept staring out of the window. CVS. Starbucks. RadioShack. McDonald's. Open field. The turn signal clicked as Bouba turned into a sprawling suburban housing subdivision.

It was starkly different from our neighborhood in Hyattsville. The houses were imposing and sat on manicured lawns. Shiny and fancy cars sat in every driveway. Someone walked a small, white furred dog on the sidewalk. A sprinkler methodically spritzed water on a lawn. He pulled up in front a red brick house. There, too, a spotless car politely sat in the driveway. Aunty Kadiatou greeted us at the door. She was a strongly built woman, and one could tell right away by looking at her that she was made of sterner stuff. Her house was enveloped in a subtle incense scent. The living room was decked with leather furniture and decorated with paintings. Her china cabinet filled with delicate plates made me think of the contrast with Mrs. Kaba's cabinet with all the figurines and other superfluous things. We exchanged greetings for what could easily have been twenty minutes, and she welcomed us to her home. She served us a hot tchiep with fish on a large mahogany dining table, and I ate like I hadn't in a very long time.

"Your tchiep tastes just like back home, Aunty," I complimented.

"Thank you, darling. I hope you make delicious meals for my son-in-law," she said teasingly, tapping Bouba on his shoulder.

"Of course, she does," Bouba replied politely.

"Well, the good thing is that now we can find all the ingredients from home right at our fingertips. When I came here in the eighties, you couldn't find anything unless you brought it with you. How times have changed. I think that you have quite a few African stores in your area."

"Yes, we have a couple of stores near us in Takoma Park," Bouba said. "I will take you," he added immediately when I looked at him.

"How are you adapting, Amina?" She asked, looking at me softly.

"I am doing okay, Aunty."

"It is not easy, I know; it is a big adjustment. Have you started working?" she asked, looking at both of us.

"I have not yet," I answered.

"Well, you should come to my salon in DC. Do you know how to braid hair?"

"No, I do not..."

"You can learn; most of my girls started with no skills at all. What do you say, mon beau?" she said, addressing Bouba.

"Sure, I don't see why not," he responded courteously.

"It would be good for you," she said, looking back at me. "It is not too far from Hyattsville, and you can start earning a little income. I started as a simple braider, but now I own the salon. I work at the hospital at night, and at the salon during the day or sometimes at our convenience store, but my husband mostly manages that business."

"How do you manage two jobs, or almost three, I should say?" I asked her.

"Darling, in America you find a way to manage!" she laughed. "I mostly supervise the girls at the salon now. I do not do much braiding, only by appointment, so I can take a nap and rest from my night job."

"I will be starting English classes soon. Could I come after school?" I queried.

"Of course! My daughter goes to Howard University, and she comes to the salon some afternoons and when she is free on the weekends. That should not be a problem." I suddenly became very glad that we had visited her and internally kicked myself for not doing so sooner. She packed a couple of Tupperware full of tchiep to take with us when we were ready to leave.

The man flipped through my files. It was a constant thing those days. I inevitably found myself at a window, looking at someone while they checked my papers to make sure they were complete. First at the embassy in Conakry, then at the Social Security Administration, then at the Motor Vehicle Department, and now I was in front of an admission officer at the English language school. I had to pass an English proficiency exam called a TOEFL exam, a test of English as a foreign language, that I would need to take in order to enroll into a university, so I had to properly learn the language and prepare for the test. I was enrolled in the A2 level class after a short assessment. Bouba wrote a check for $850 to cover the first half of the course, which ran for eight weeks, making it clear that it was a loan I would repay him once I started working. I converted the amount to Guinean francs, and it took a minute to get over my shock. That was more than a full year's tuition at a private school back home. At that moment, however, I could care less; I just wanted to be registered as that would get me a step closer to enrolling in college. However, I had to figure out how I would pay for school fees moving forward, I thought.

On the first day of school, I got lost in the building looking for my classroom, and I was late for my first course, Basic Vocabulary, Grammar, and Pronunciation. Our teacher was a tall blond woman from North Dakota who had moved to Washington, DC, to teach English as a second language to foreign students. She told us that the first rule of class was "English only." It did not matter how we put the words together; the important thing was to communicate everything in English, and we would get to conjugation and sentence building later. If we did not know how to say a word, the shelf was lined with dual language dictionaries, she added as she handed us our textbooks. We sat in a circle, introduced ourselves to each other, and shared an interesting fact about ourselves using English only. We shared a lot of laughs as we all took our turn butchering our way through. I made two new friends by lunchtime, one from Brazil and another from Malaysia.

I finished my classes at 2 p.m. and took the metro to head to Aunty Kadiatou's salon. I had printed out the step-by-step directions from MapQuest earlier, and I looked at it again to confirm my stop. I exited the subway at the Georgia Avenue-Petworth station and walked out onto a busy street. I looked at nearby buildings for reference and followed the street. It did not take me long to spot the sign: Kadiatou Hair Braiding.

"Hey there...you made it!" Aunty Kadiatou cheered as soon as I pushed the door open. The hair salon was buzzing with activity. There were customers in every chair getting their hair braided.

"Everyone, this is Amina; she is our new recruit." The whole group stopped talking and looked in my direction, but none of the girls said anything except the one sitting closest to the door.

"Hi," she said as she looked me up and down. All the others had gone back to their talking and braiding, their heads tilted toward the television. There was a Nigerian movie on, and the volume must have been on maximum because they almost had to yell to communicate.

"You can put your bag here," Aunty Kadiatou called from behind the counter. I walked behind the counter and found a shelf to sit my book bag on. A few purses were thrown on the shelves among food in plastic containers, a panoply of plastic bags filled with stuff, and a prayer mat. I looked around. The large bay window facing the street was plastered with posters of braids models, the women on the pictures smiling brightly as their braid crowns shone. There was a black leather couch pushed against the window and a small table adorned with hair magazines. Packs of hair extensions for sale were pegged on the wall behind the counter. There were eight customer chairs, and the braiders sat around them on high stools, sometimes with two braiders to one customer. There was hair on the floor around the chairs, the paint was peeling on some parts of the ceiling, and the whole place smelled of damp carpet. I was surprised at the divergence of the place's atmosphere from its owner's home.

"The bathroom is in the back," Aunty Kadiatou said. "This is Sira; she is from Guinea, too." She said pointing at the girl who had greeted me. "Next to her is Francine, she is from Cameroon; Hawa and Binta and Fatou are from Guinea as well; Ndeye over there is from Senegal; and this is the trouble row," she said teasingly, pointing to the other side, "Amandine, Bintou, Mireille, and Fanta are from the Ivory Coast." They all laughed. "You can start by sweeping the floor. You will find the broom behind the bathroom door. When you're done, grab a mannequin head on the shelf and bring it here so I can show you how to fix a basic braid."

I spent the rest of the afternoon learning how to affix an extension braid and how to properly braid it straight without knots. Aunty Kadiatou told me to take the mannequin head home to keep practicing, and once she was satisfied with the quality of the braids, I could start assisting the main braiders. There was a system in the remuneration. The braiding fee was split between the salon owner and the braider. The person who affixed the braids pocketed a larger portion of the fee than the one who finished it out. When two braiders styled a customer's hair, the person who braided the front of the head made more than the one who did the back because the braids in the front required smaller sectioning. She explained the different styles: micro braids, single braids, Senegalese twists, kinky twists, box braids, cornrows, and so on. The prices were set based on style, length of hair, and size of braids. I nearly fell off my chair when she said that the starting charge for a micro braids style was $180 and could go upward to $400. On a slow week, I could go home with three hundred dollars after a split, and on a busy week, I could take upward of six hundred. It all depended on how fast I worked. Even on a slow week, you would beat minimum wage if you apply yourself, she concluded. Those amounts sounded enormous to me who had never earned a penny in my life. I could not believe that I could possibly be making that much money, and even less that such an underrated skill back home was such a hot commodity in America. That night after dinner, I sat in front of the TV, the mannequin head pressed between my legs, a pack of hair extensions on the couch arm, and I practiced until my fingers were sore.

I fell into my new routine pretty easily. Bouba and I drove to the metro station together every morning, and then we went our separate ways. He sometimes let me drive after we practiced a few times in the Home Depot parking lot. I went to my classes for the first half of the day, then headed to the hair salon in the afternoon. I had started the habit of planning my weekly meals on the weekends, and I, too, had started freezing prepared meals. I was horrified at the idea at first but soon realized that it tasted all the same after a long day anyway, and it made my life much easier. I met Aunty Kadiatou's daughter, Salimata, on my third day at the salon. She dropped by after her classes, and we hit it off right away. Her Pular and French were a little broken, and so was my English, but we found a medium somewhere between the three languages. She was born in the US and had never been to Guinea. She was planning on taking a trip there after graduation, so she asked me a thousand questions about it. The other girls gossiped and cackled all the time. They had warmed up a little to me, but there was still a small rift between us, and I could not understand why until Salimata explained that they had treated her the same way at first, and later understood that they somehow envied her for having the opportunity to go to school. They often mocked us when we sat in the corner and completed assignments during downtime. It bothered me at first, but Salimata told me not to mind them.

Their favorite topic of conversation was men. Some days, men were great, and others, they were good for nothing; it all depended on their mood and what one of them was going through with their boyfriend or husband at that moment in time. The consensus from all of them, however, was that women needed to make their own money, especially so that they did not need to depend on a man in this country. No one could dictate to them what they did with their lives. Few of them had actually come to the United States through arranged marriages, but none of them had worked out and had ended in separation or divorce. The men sometimes tried to control them and kept them from leaving the house, or in Ndeye's case, her husband took all the money she made at the salon and beat her if she spoke up. I reflected on it and concluded that I was actually lucky. My situation was not ideal but nowhere as dire as what I was hearing from these girls. Most of them now lived together as roommates to save on the cost of housing. They were all building houses back home or supporting the families they had left behind. Bouba also sent a portion of his income home every month through Western Union or through friends traveling to Guinea. In the background of their discussions, there was always a Nollywood movie playing on the television. A man came into the salon every week selling DVDs of the newest Nigerian movies or delivering the long-awaited parts five or six of some movie franchise. I always felt it was rude how the braiders talked loudly over the heads of the customers, sometimes criticizing their hair in dialects. I did not understand how Aunty Kadiatou could sleep in that ruckus. She often laid down on the black sofa if she did not have a customer and started snoring shortly after.

The majority of the clientele was African American women, though there were the occasional Caucasian women or Black men who wanted cornrows done to their hair. I was amazed at how we looked so alike—big hipped, full lipped, cheerful—yet we were so culturally different from each other. Occasionally, we had Nigerian or Ghanaian customers. I admired how they looked completely integrated in American life. According to the braiders, it was because they came from English-speaking countries, and beyond the shared language, they also shared somewhat similar values and religion with people in the US, so it was not as hard for them to assimilate into American life and ethos. They often came to the United States on student visas, scholarships, or through family reunification. I was curious about their lives and sometimes wanted to start conversations with them but did not because they were often engrossed in a book or had earpieces on, but also because I was still self-conscious about my level of English.

My life was full but fragmented. It was as if I were living in three separate worlds. At school, I studied and learned about American values, principles, and philosophy, and I interacted with a diverse group of people. There were so many students of different nationalities, and it was stimulating to meet and engage with people from all over the world. We found many interesting things to talk about, and I ended up sharing a lot about my own culture and traditions because most of the students I met had no idea about Africa in general, let alone a small country on the western coast of Africa called Guinea. I felt ashamed about my arranged marriage, so I withheld that piece of information. We shared stories about our experiences in America so far, like the one student from Senegal who shook everyone's hand in the classroom on his first day of school as everyone looked on confused or horrified, because in his culture it was rude to enter a room and not shake everyone's hand. At the salon, it was as if I were back in Africa, with the loudness, the shared code, the food, the stories, and the belly laughs; and at home, I was the lost, confused, but dutiful Amina who catered to her husband. I sometimes chatted with Fatima late into the night, making sure Bouba was fast asleep before I slid in on my side of the bed, wishing that the next day would come fast so that I could return to my other lives.

The snow melted, the leaves turned green, the summer heat turned the lawns yellow, and the leaves started turning orange. I had a hard time getting accustomed to the long summer days; it was strange looking outside at nine in the evening and still see a glimpse of the sun setting. Then the days were becoming shorter again, and the sun was less scorching. I passed my TOEFL exam, and after a strenuous application process, I was accepted into the University of Maryland. With the help of Salimata, I completed my application, wrote an essay, and sent my high school diploma and transcripts to a local company to obtain certified translations. I wrote to Ms. Tawel to ask for a letter of recommendation, and she was elated to hear that I was enrolling in college. At last, I was going to start my studies. I was well settled into my life. After sending my first paycheck to Aunty and Ousbi, I saved every penny I made and deposited it into a checking account I opened at Bank of America. It would come in handy because I had missed the deadline to apply for financial aid for my school tuition.

I glanced up at the electronic board to check when the next train would be arriving. I did not want to be late to my orientation at the university. Being in the subway station during rush hour was a curious thing. The halls and the platforms were packed to the brim; people rushed, ran after trains, and took the escalator two steps at a time sometimes, yet you did not hear one single voice. Everything was silent except for the sound of footsteps on the tiles and the trains entering and leaving the station. If you closed your eyes, you would think that a herd of sheep was running through the tunnels.

The day was hectic but exciting. I met with my counselor, registered for my first semester courses, met other new freshmen, and went on a tour of the campus. I was eager to start my classes. I did not go to the salon that afternoon since I finished at the campus after four, and I was supposed to meet Bouba at the Takoma Park station to do our weekly shopping at the African store. The sky was getting cloudy by the time I exited the subway station. I spotted Bouba as I approached the parking lot. I more than often wondered what was going on in his head and why he was so closed off. All he cared about was his work, and he was oblivious to anything else around him, or at least he pretended to be. Our relationship had not progressed an inch from when it had first started; if anything, it had regressed. I shopped around the store while Bouba gathered the big items—the packs of water and the twenty-five-kilo bag of rice. I picked up yams, cassava, plantains, Maggi cubes, and ogiri, going through my mental notes and trying not to forget anything. I couldn't get out of the habit of converting dollars to Guinean francs, and some of the prices were astronomical compared to what they were at the market back home, but since I could not avoid buying it, I just picked it up and dropped it in my cart. The checkout line was long, and the cashier chatted up every customer, slowly bagging their items. The wind had picked up when we walked outside. I helped Bouba load the groceries in the trunk, and he walked away to return the cart to the store. I was pushing the water to the back of the trunk when I saw some movement out of the corner of my eye and looked up. A woman was standing next to me. I was confused when I stepped back and looked at her. She was staring at me, and the little boy who held her hand was also looking at me. Her skin was a smooth chocolate tone, her face was nicely made up, and she wore a rich lipstick the color of red wine. Her weave was as long as the Fatala River, flowing down her back. She wore blue jeans, a leather jacket, and knee-high boots. We stared at each other in silence until she spoke slowly, dragging on each word, her tone disdainful.

"So, it is you...the little African wife." She looked me up and down as if to size me up. I looked back at her, not understanding, and fumbled to remember my English.

"I am sorry; can I help you?"

"Can you help me?!" she sneered. "No sweetie, you can't help me; I just need my man back!" My mouth dropped and my face twitched. I thought I had misheard her. She gauged my reaction, but I could not get a single word out. This must be a mistake, I thought, but her voice rose again, scratching the air.

"Oh, he didn't tell you about me? I am Tiffany! The woman he has been with for the past six years, and this is Noah, our son. We want our life back, the one we had before he brought you here! Come tell her, boo!" She flicked her hair with the back of her hand and put her hands on her hips as she glanced toward the store. I looked in that direction and saw Bouba standing on the sidewalk, petrified, gripping the car keys, looking back and forth at the woman and me. There were no words needed. I knew right then that this was no mistake. I crumpled like paper. I felt dizzy and nauseous. My heart thudded in my chest, and I felt the world recede around me. I instinctively turned around and started walking as fast as I could away from the parking lot, her voice echoing behind me.

I walked without direction, unaware of the time. The sky had opened up and was pouring out cords of rain. The bus shelter where I found refuge did not offer much of a shield against the furious elements. It was as if Mother Nature knew the turmoil that was ravaging me. I sat on the corner of the bench, curled up against the glass, waiting for the first bus to arrive so I could get away from all the madness. What in the world had that been? I kept replaying that moment over and over in my head. How could it be? How could he? Had I imagined it? I rode the bus until it stopped raining. I kept walking aimlessly until my steps led me into a Barnes and Noble where I found a chair in a corner and curled up in it until it was closing time. I couldn't go home. I wandered around the strip mall for a while before dialing Salimata's number.

Aunty Kadiatou picked me up from the train station. At her home, she sat on the sofa, and Salimata sat next to me, holding my hand. She had lent me some clothes to change into from my drenched ones. We sat in silence, letting the shock of what I had recounted to them settle in.

"I can't say I am surprised," Aunty Kadiatou finally said. I sharply looked at her.

"Sweetheart, it is a common occurrence. I have seen it happen countless times. These young men are here for a long time, and they end up being involved in relationships, sometimes for love, and other times for convenience. When the family comes calling for them to get married, they cannot easily extricate themselves from the situations they are in."

"But why keep it a secret? It is not like I was going to eat him for it!" I blurted out.

"It is not as easy as you think. How do you suppose he was going to tell his wife about this other woman? Also, his family may not know about it; actually, I am ninety-nine percent sure that they do not know. Telling you would run the risk of exposing him."

"But Mom! Still, is that an excuse?" Salimata interjected.

"Of course not, but all I am saying is that things are more complicated than they seem. I am not condoning this, but let's not lose our objectivity, either."

Salimata rolled her eyes. Aunty would have slapped me if I ever did that.

"Anyway, I am going to call him to let him know that you are here, and we can reconvene tomorrow. Get something to eat and rest your body, my child," Aunty Kadiatou concluded, picking up her phone. Why was she defending him? I thought. I was not hungry; I did not even want to think about food. Salimata and I went to her bedroom.

I stayed in bed at Aunty Kadiatou's house for two days, revisiting the prior months. It all made sense then—the emotional and physical distance, the lack of engagement, the reason why he wouldn't come close to me, the empty closet, the exactly numbered set of dishes. It was because he had another life, but how had he carried this on for all those months? It was even harder to face my own hypocrisy. I had not married him because I loved him or because I particularly wanted to be with him. I had married him because I saw him as a gateway to something I desired, so what right did I have to judge? Still, I felt a nagging feeling that wouldn't go away. Maybe I had started believing the whole charade. He came over the following day, but I refused to leave the bedroom. I was not ready to see him. Aunty Kadiatou, concerned, came to the bedroom and asked me to come outside for just a few minutes for some fresh air and to have a bite to eat, but I did not have the energy. On the third day, Salimata snatched the sheets off me and told me to get up and take a shower. The water did me some good. I turned my phone on and saw more than a dozen missed calls from Bouba, Aunty, and Fatima. I checked my text messages. There were several messages; the last one was from Fatima.

I can't reach you. I am worried. Call me.

I sighed and walked out to the deck. The air was cool, and I shivered as I sat down on the metallic chair to make some phone calls. Fatima was stunned. She wanted to catch the next bus out of Montreal and come over, but I told her that was not necessary; besides she would have to miss work, and I knew that she needed the money for her tuition. She had been accepted to a university in Montreal, and she worked part-time to supplement the money her parents sent her for school fees. Aunty Kadiatou had already told Aunty Hassanatou what had happened while I was holed up in the bedroom. So much for his secret, I thought. She pressed me to return home; the rest would be discussed later.

"You should not have left," she admonished me on the other end of the line. "You made a big deal out of something small. Is she the one he is married to? Is she the one in the house? Is she the one that his family chose for him? Don't be foolish. Don't you know that men stray? You haven't even heard from him; for all you know, they may not even be together."

I pulled the phone away from my ear and actually stared at it for a moment, dumbfounded. What was she talking about? She had not been there; she had not seen what happened. How could she possibly know? "Does the fact that I am in *his house* as *his wife* eliminate the staggering truth that he has a son with a woman he was, and probably still is, in a relationship with?" I retorted to her. I had never raised my voice at Aunty, but at that moment, it was the last of my concerns.

"What does it matter? That son was born out of sin, so he does not count. He could never dare bring that child in front of his parents!"

"How does a child, a human being of flesh and blood, not count, Aunty?"

"You have been living there for a few months and already you are thinking and talking like a toubab. You need to come back home!" I suddenly felt tired all over again, so I hung up and went back to bed. The anger was seeping through my bones, through my skin, turning into droplets of cold sweat under the cover. His mother called me the next day. The news had traveled. She went on for a whole half hour. "My son has brought shame to our family, but I hope you can get over the deceit and please return home. Please, my child, let bygones be bygones; let's move forward, and we will sort through this together." I turned off my phone again. I needed to think. I stayed for two more days before I decided to return to the apartment. I sensed that I had overstayed my welcome; besides, I needed to wear my own clothes, and my classes were starting in a couple of days.

Chapter Thirteen

On the way back home, my thoughts crystallized into something slightly more coherent. I felt weary, but I knew I had to do something; I just didn't know what yet. When I arrived home, Bouba was sitting on the couch, his head resting in the palms of his hands. He jumped off the sofa when I opened the door.

"Amina, thank god you are here!" he said, stepping forward. I took a step back and he stopped. He ran his hand over his head before speaking again.

"Can we talk, please?"

I remained silent. He walked back to the sofa to sit down.

"Please let's talk, hear me out..." I walked over to the dinette, pulled out a chair, and crossed my arms when I sat down.

"I am so sorry, Amina. I was going to tell you; I did not know that Tiffany was going to do that." He waited for a reaction that did not come, so he continued.

"I did not know how to bring it up; it has been eating me alive, trust me. I couldn't tell you back in Guinea because I did not know you yet, and I was not sure how you would react. We met when I was in college, and we've been together since. She helped me out a lot in the first years."

"Do you love her?"

"We have been together for six years," he replied meekly.

"That does not answer the question," I snapped back. He looked down and murmured, "Yes."

I paused for a moment.

"Then why go through the whole marriage thing? Why did you get me mixed up in this?"

"Come on, Amina, you know how things go with our traditions. I had stalled my parents for long enough, and I was backed into a corner and could no longer say no. We talked about it, remember? I was under the impression that we had an understanding."

"Yes, but you forgot to mention one enormous detail."

"And I have told you why, and for that I am so sorry!"

"So, what now, Bouba?" He did not answer right away and stared at his feet. I repeated my question, "Bouba, what now?"

"I don't know what to do. All I know is that my family would shred me to pieces if I even attempted to end this marriage, yet I cannot erase Tiffany and Noah out of my life; they are part of me."

"So, what then? We are supposed to live in this sham marriage?" I yelled at him.

His words stung me although I did not understand why they did. It was self-contradictory. We had never really had a romantic life; it was in fact just that from the get-go—a sham marriage. But I had grown used to him, I saw him as a part of *my* life, and now there were two new people in the equation. I guess I had unconsciously and naively hoped that there would be something, that we would grow our dysfunctional relationship into a real connection somehow. I felt ashamed to admit it to myself. Me, who didn't even want to be in the relationship in the first place. But Bouba had been kind to me, and I had grown fond of him in my own twisted way. He got up from the sofa, pulled a chair next to me, and leaned in.

"Amina, listen to me. You see when my parents applied pressure on me to get married, I told them that I would do it, but the condition was that the girl had to be in school already. I knew that I would be called to bring whoever I marry back to the US with me, and I wanted whoever I ended up marrying to get something out of it, because the woman usually gets the short end of the stick in these situations. What I am saying is, I want you to study, I want you to build a future for yourself, I want you to be happy, I want you to find interests in life, and I will help you with that. I will do whatever it takes to push you in that direction, but I just can't give you my heart." We stared at each other in silence. Ha, and I thought I had been pulling the reins. So much for controlling the narrative.

"So, is that why you've been so nice to me?" I finally muttered.

"No, Amina, I am nice to you because you deserve it, and that is what people do. Be nice to each other, especially when they live together."

I struggled to push the words out, so they came out distorted.

"And that is why you will not be intimate with me?"

"Amina, you are beautiful girl, smart, with a personality to fill this whole place…"

"But? Because there certainly is a *but*, right?"

He paused. "But…being with you physically feels like I am cheating on Tiffany. That one night in Conakry, I just couldn't control my urges, and I am sorry to have put you in that situation." He really loved her.

"So, why the fuss about there being no blood? What did it matter then?" I felt anger rise up in me again.

"That was just a stupid thing to say. I was feeling guilty, so I took it out on you. Sorry again."

"For the record, I was a virgin," I snapped at him.

"I do not doubt it one bit, Amina. And for the record, it did not and does not matter to me. This whole thing..." He sighed, waving his hand in the air as if to dismiss something. "...it is not you; it is not anything you did. It is all me. I just hope we can find a way to move forward." He looked resigned.

"I do not see how right now." It came out of my lips like a heavy lament.

"Can we think on it?" He said, taking both my hands in his. What was there to think about? There was a quasi-wife and a whole son out there. Tiffany. Tiffany with the long weave and the red lips. I remembered the scene in the parking lot and pulled my hands back.

"What have you been telling her? How could you explain my presence?" I asked him, genuinely curious. He let out a long sigh and leaned back.

"Do you really want to know?" he said, shaking his head, letting his arms fall to the sides of the chair.

"I actually do, as strange as it may seem."

He explained to me how his life had been disrupted by the incessant calls and cries from his mother to go home and get married. He admitted that he just did not have the strength to face his parents, specifically his mother, and say no, especially when they had sacrificed a lot to get him to where he was. When he couldn't take the stress anymore, he told Tiffany everything. It created a rift in their relationship at first, but they eventually reconciled. He was torn for months, but he had to be a good son. So, he decided to get married, but they agreed that the marriage would be platonic; they had a plan. He would bring the girl over, help her get settled and guide her in setting up a life for herself while he slowly extracted himself from the marriage. He would tell his parents that he had tried. But she did not expect that it would take so many months. She did not expect that he would spend every night away, only getting a few stolen hours with him while she remained in the dark like a petty criminal, a mistress hidden in the shadows. He had confessed to her about being intimate just once, and she had gone off the deep end and decided to end the farce. They had thought it was a good plan at the time.

"And now you've made a big mess," I said, shaking my head.

"Why did you bring me over?" I continued. "Your life would have been much easier if you hadn't; you could have led your double life without anyone even knowing."

"Trust me, I know many people who do, but it would not be fair to you, Amina."

I should have been preoccupied by me, by my seething feelings. I should have hated him, but I felt sad for him. I was not sure how long we sat there in silence, trying to find an answer to the question that was dancing around us, taunting us: "Now what?" At some point, I went to the kitchen and opened the fridge to get a drink, but it was almost empty. I opened the kitchen cabinet, and it was also almost bare. I looked at him inquiringly, and he understood right away. The groceries were still in the trunk of the car.

We did not find a solution that night or the following days. Things were somewhat cordial between us; however, I couldn't help but feel a hindrance, a tension, like a helium balloon about to burst. I could not see it or touch it, but I felt it. Nevertheless, we just carried on and tried to sort through the sordid facts of our life. I did not tell Aunty about my conversation with Bouba, and he was still sorting out the recent developments with his family, but I was sure he left out the part about the plan he and that woman had concocted. I heard his muffled voice through the closed bedroom door. He used to talk to his mother in front of me, but he now took the phone to the bedroom or bathroom. They talked for hours. I imagined her melodramatic reactions on the other side of the line. Did she really not know at all? I wondered. I couldn't pinpoint what I was feeling at first, but it must have been relief, because as the days came and went, the heaviness of the air dissipated, and I felt lighter. I grasped that I did not have to be tied to Bouba. A door had opened for me to leave my marriage. I did not have to remain a wife to someone I had not chosen, someone who it turned out didn't want to be me with me, either. In the meantime, we carried on and did those things people do to divert themselves from their existence.

The start of my classes was a welcome distraction.

The first week, or syllabus week as it was called, was quite interesting—the professors were engaging, and the students came from all walks of life. It took me a couple of weeks to adjust to the layout of the campus, figure out where to get coffee and food, and how much time it took me to get from one class to the other on the opposite side of campus. The long and full days I had back in high school were a thing of the past. On my busiest days, I had three classes. I had been lucky to find classes that were all in the morning, as my neighbor in accounting class had four hours to kill until his next class. I was not sure what I would major in, but I was leaning toward a business major. I still had time to decide, I thought. I used the money I had earned and saved from the hair salon to pay for a portion of my tuition until I could apply for financial aid. I found a new home in my community at school among my classmates, the Black Student Union, and the African Student Association. I loved seeing all of the diversity coming from the African continent, from Algeria to Zimbabwe, and I felt comfortable in that circle. I occasionally got the witless comment from my fellow American students about Africans living in trees, or having lions for pets. I sometimes indulged them and made up stories about the jungle I lived in while I laughed inwardly, but more than often I just brushed it off and ascribed it to ignorance. When I went to the salon after school, Aunty Kadiatou asked me about the situation at home, and I evasively told her that everything was fine.

She shot me a side eye but did not comment further. She knew I was not telling the truth, but I appreciated her for not inquiring further. Aunty called more often, and we talked briefly, but she was happy that I had gone back to Bouba's house and had not created a scandal. Her calls were poorly disguised checkups to ensure that things had not degenerated overnight. It was most baffling that she cared more about appearances than my well-being. At the end of my long days, I prayed and talked to my mother while I lay in bed. I hoped that from somewhere in the universe, she could see and hear me. Look, Neneh, your little girl is in college now.

The days were getting colder, night was falling earlier, and I was confused by daylight saving time. I didn't know you could spring forward time, and reel it back, but I had stopped asking some questions. My new routine was on solid footing, so I decided to get a second job. I started filling out applications in restaurants and retail stores in the vicinity of the college campus and the hair salon. I needed to earn more money. I needed to make enough to be able to send some back home, save some, and eventually support myself. "You will wear yourself out!" Salimata said, but I did not care; it was a necessity. I did not tell her this, but I believed that we were in different situations. She lived at home with her parents, and I would soon find myself alone, left to fend for myself. I would work evenings, overnights, weekends if I had to. I filled out applications in a myriad of places, but when

I followed up, the answer was always the same: "We are sorry, but we went with another candidate. Good luck with your search!" I couldn't help but think that it had something to do with my heavy accent because folding clothes or stocking shelves did not require extraordinary skills. My English had improved considerably, but it was mired with a heavy West African and French accent, which made it difficult for some people to understand me clearly. Going through the drive-through was sometimes an unnerving mission. I practiced with Salimata to perfect the American accent, but that was easier said than done. I sometimes envied how the words rolled so easily off her tongue and came out sounding just right. I was starting to lose hope when one day, on my way to the salon, I spotted a sign on a Popeyes window: Hiring Event—On-the-Spot Interviews. What was there to lose? I walked in and asked for a manager. I interviewed with a man wearing a hairnet and a mustache that kept distracting me. I walked out twenty minutes later with a job and a starting date scribbled on a post-it note.

"Everyone! Gather around!" a strong, ebullient voice called out. A couple dozen students from the university's Black Student Union had showed up to a volunteering event in commemoration of Dr. Martin Luther King, Jr. Day of Service. I had recently started my second semester at the University. We all dozily started moving; it was still very early. The temperatures were freezing, and I wished we could gather up inside instead of the parking lot. The voice belonged to a tall, young man wearing a red Terrapins baseball cap, standing on a crate. His voice was commanding as he thanked us for coming and gave us some guidelines on the planned activities. The community center where we were volunteering had received multiple donations, and they were all stored in a large warehouse next to the parking lot. Our job for the day was to sort through the articles by category. He butchered my name when he called me from the list. I was assigned with two other students to sort several bundles of clothes; others were assigned to sorting through household items, canned foods, packs of water, and other staples. We made our way to the warehouse, where we organized and folded the items in several piles—T-shirts, socks, pants, shorts, and so on. The atmosphere was jovial despite the cold and dampness in the warehouse. Someone put some music on, and we rocked to the Black Eyed Peas, Rihanna, and Justin Timberlake. We "leaned wit it and rocked wit it" to Dem Franchize Boyz until the early afternoon.

A late lunch was organized after our volunteering event, and we all congregated around a few tables that had been pulled together at a diner nearby. I was looking at the menu when someone pulled out a chair and sat next to me. I didn't recognize him at first without his baseball cap but did as soon as he spoke. He had removed his jacket and was wearing jeans and a grey shirt, whose sleeves he had rolled up to his elbows. His skin color reminded me of the smooth brown shell of the shea butter nut.

"Thank you for coming today, we really appreciate it!" he said, addressing me.

"Sure," I replied to him.

"I am Enoch. I don't think I have seen you around before. What's your name again?"

"Aminatou. I go by Amina."

"I will call you Amy," he said facetiously. I faced him and took a good look at him before replying. I was taken aback for a moment by his striking features.

"My name is Amina!" I said, exasperated.

"Okay, Amy!" he laughed. I was not amused. "Nice to meet you! Where are you from?"

"Guinea," I said reluctantly.

"Well, thank you Aminatou from Guinea for showing up today. Every pair of hands counts, and I hope you enjoy your lunch!" He said my name right that time, and with that, he was gone. I was annoyed by him, but at the same time, my curiosity was piqued. I wanted to know who he was. I stole glances at him at the other end of the table throughout lunch, and I quickly looked away when he caught me looking at him. Some students decided to go to the ice-skating rink after lunch, but I chose to go home. I hadn't had a free day in a long time, and I was planning on spending the rest of it in bed.

The hours were grueling. I worked the late-night and weekend shifts at Popeyes. This was not the salon. I learned to stay on my feet for hours, serving hungry, sometimes cranky, and rude customers while a supervisor always looked on. I came home every night with my back aching, my legs numb, and smelling like fried chicken as if I were also rubbed in seasoning and dumped in the fryer with the other pieces of chicken legs, thighs, and wings. I scrubbed the smell off of me in the shower and rubbed myself with scented lotions, but it seemed stayed with me even though I knew it really wasn't there. I was shocked when I received my first paycheck. I stared at it, not comprehending. I had calculated how much money I would be making per pay period based on the rate I had been told when I was offered the job, and the amount I was looking at was nowhere near it. Bouba laughed a half laugh, trying to smother it because we were still on thin ground. Taxes. "Once again, welcome to America," he said. He explained the concept of gross and net pay, tax withholdings and deductions. All that work for that little money, and then Uncle Sam took a big chunk of it. I felt defeated before I had even started climbing the mountain, but I was not doing this for kicks; I had to keep going until I at least found something better, especially now that I knew I would have to pay taxes on my earnings at the salon during my annual filing. The American Dream was creeping further away from me, and the road to it was becoming much longer.

Chapter Fourteen

Bouba did not come home one night. I was surprised at my indifference. He sent me a text message explaining something about an emergency at work, but I knew that it was just a pretext, a cover or a ruse for Tiffany. I also knew that from that moment on, things would be irreparably different; the nail was in the coffin, and the whole thing was headed downward from there. What did we have in common anyway beyond a roof and a chaste bed? I called Fatima and we chatted until I drifted off to sleep. I woke up in the middle of the night with my heart beating out of my chest. I could not go back to sleep for the rest of the night.

The air held the promise of a frigid day when I stepped outside the next morning. I called Aunty from the bus station, and before she could even place a word, I calmly said, "I want to divorce Bouba." There was a long pause before her voice came through, uncertain.

"What nonsense is this, Amina?"

"How does it work? Do I call Uncle Abdul? Or do I just tell Bouba?" I continued, ignoring her question. She drew out a long breath.

"Amina, what is going on? Are you two fighting?"

"We are not fighting. I just want a divorce," I said evenly.

"You are not making any sense! You can't just wake up one morning and decide that you want a divorce!" Her voice was growing impatient.

"Yes, I can!" I was stunned at my own boldness. "I can't do this anymore. It is all a farce. Aunty, please, I want you to take me seriously for once. I need out; how do I do it?"

"You want to ruin your life? What has gotten into you? Is that what you want to do? You want to be a pariah?" She was yelling at this point.

"I think that would be preferable to what is happening now. I can't pretend anymore. Even he can't pretend anymore; what is the point of dragging this out?"

"Because you are not putting in enough effort, Amina! If you put in as much effort as when you complain about it, your marriage would be fine! You are not the first girl to be in an arranged marriage, and you won't be the last. It is not magic; you work to make it work. Since you arrived, if you had gotten pregnant, divorce would not be the word on your lips right now, but you are stubborn, Amina. You found a man from a respectable family who went through hoops to marry you. The woman is the one who carries the marriage and takes everything on; she has to be blind, deaf and mute..." I pulled the phone away from my ear for an instant as she continued her tirade. What hoops? I had been basically offered up on a platter. And get pregnant? I laughed out loud.

"Hello? Hello?" I brought the phone back to my ear.

"Aunty, you do not know everything."

"Yes, I do know everything because I have been through it too, Amina!"

"No Aunty, I really mean there are some things you do not know."

She stopped talking for a moment. "What do you mean?"

"He has only touched me once since we have been married, Aunty. Once, in over a year! We live like brother and sister; besides, he told me himself that he can never commit his heart to me because it belongs to someone else. He did not come home last night. I don't even care that he did not come home, but why is everything always about what I did or did not do—what about him, Aunty? What about my welfare? What about my pride? What about my self-worth? Why do I have to keep subjecting myself to this? The woman is always the one taking everything on. What if she can't anymore? What if she doesn't want to carry it anymore; what if she is exhausted, Aunty?" I yelled back at her. I did not realize that tears had started rolling down my cheeks. The bus arrived then, but I did not get on it. There was a long silence on the other side of the line. Maybe from the shock. Shock that I had actually yelled at her, or shock from what I had told her, but when she finally spoke, her voice was grave.

"You never told me that, Amina."

I nodded as if she could see me and wiped the tears from my eyes.

"That changes things, but still, Amina, that is not a reason to jump to divorce. In our culture there are men who are married to several wives, you know that, and the not-touching-you part is something that can be…" I interrupted her mid-sentence. I could not take it anymore. I could not listen to one more word. I could not listen to any more rationalizations.

"I have to go, Aunty." And I hung up the phone. I spent a few minutes pulling myself back together again before dialing Koto's number. I got his voicemail. I made a mental note to myself to call him again later. I was considerably late to class. I did not want to open the door and cross the room to find a seat while everyone looked on, so I went to the library. I was there for a short time when I saw Mr. Ronald walking toward me. He was one of those nontraditional students, like me. He was an older veteran who had decided to go back to school to get his degree. I often saw him at our association gatherings.

"Hey Amina, can I sit with you?" he said in his deep voice.

"Sure," I said, making space for him, although I would have rather been alone. He threw his backpack on the floor and sat down.

"What are you studying right now?" he asked.

"Nothing in particular, just doing some advance reading for my next class."

"Oh, I will do the same. I didn't have class today, but I had to get out of the missus's hair." He pulled out a couple of heavy books from his backpack. We ended up not doing any reading. He liked to talk, so he told me about his life, about his dogs, about his wife who had decided to start working again—the only problem being she worked from home, so he could no longer watch TV with the volume loud or do anything else without tiptoeing around. When he took a pause to breathe, he looked at me and asked brusquely, "Do you have a boyfriend?"

I looked up.

"Of course, a pretty young girl like you has a boyfriend," he added almost to himself.

"You can say so—I am married."

"Oh wow, really?" he exclaimed. "You look pretty young to be married already."

"I am. It was arranged."

"Oh, I see." I was not sure why I was telling him this, but I did not have time to think on it.

"So, does it feel strange to be a young college student and be married?" I'll admit it was a fact that I did not share with the other students because it made me feel uncomfortable. I did not want to be asked questions I could not answer, and I was worried that I would be judged or would hear uninvited opinions. College life in America meant freedom, dating, new experiences, and drinking, none of which were part of my life, bar the new experiences, though they were a different type of new experience than the average American's. The rest did not fit in my life.

"Does it feel strange to be an older college student and be married?" I finally asked, smiling. He laughed.

"Touché!" I held my book up conspicuously, passively showing that I was going back to reading, but he kept talking.

"Your marriage was arranged? Well, good for you guys!"

"Huh?" I look at him, surprised.

"Well, yes...surprising coming from an old, white American guy?" He smiled. "You see, here in America we have a blessing that can also be a curse. We have too much choice. Too many choices of what or where to eat, what to wear, what to buy, who to date, and so on."

"But isn't that a good thing?"

"It is a great thing, that is why I said it is a blessing,

182

but it can sometimes turn into a curse. See, because we have so much choice, it is driving us insane. I hope that your marriage is a good one, but in choosing for you, your parents relieved you of a huge responsibility and stress. Here, people are free to date whomever they want, and however many people they want. It is all about love, but love can be found and thrown out like a piece of Kleenex with the OkCupids and Match.coms of this world. People are looking for their soul mates and getting into relationships blindly, confident that it will succeed, but the multiple options to find love and the potential interests that are a click away make building these relationships very difficult, if not impossible. I know because my daughters are trapped in this vicious loop. So, people get caught up in a string of meaningless relationships and rushed breakups, trying to find that elusive perfect love...and trust me, I am an old guy—perfect love is a myth. I quite frankly feel bad for these young people."

"But how is having someone arbitrarily chosen for you any better?" I retorted.

"I think that parents would never willingly put their children in harm's way, and their choosing a spouse for a child is based on the fact that they have probably experienced it themselves, and they are basing their decisions on their own experience. They are possibly afraid of the unknown, because a love marriage is in fact unknown to them."

"Wouldn't putting their child in a relationship with about a total stranger also be an unknown for their daughter or son?" I replied, a little irked.

"I have known quite a few people in your situation from different parts of the world, if you can believe it, and overall they seem okay with it and are happy." He opened a water bottle and took a sip.

"Well, maybe it is just a front. I don't think most people would tell someone if they were unhappy. I can't see how a woman can be happy with choices being made for her and not by her," I responded, fixing my eyes on him.

"You are looking at it only from the woman's standpoint; the men are also entering an arranged marriage."

"I can only confidently speak from my point of view."

"All I am saying is, it is possible to be happy in an arranged marriage as long as you were not forced. I have seen it."

"Are you in an arranged marriage, Mr. Ronald?" I could never bring myself to just calling him Ronald like the other students. It did not seem right.

"No, I am not...but wait, do not dismiss my argument because I have not personally experienced the subject at hand."

"Well, it is hard to comment on skydiving if you never leave the plane, wouldn't you say? Are you a woman, Mr. Ronald?"

"Okay, okay...I see where this is going," he said, smiling.

"Are you a young woman who just wanted to live her

life, who wanted to have the freedom to dream about her own future, but instead who finds herself waking up every morning next to a person she barely knows, who does not share anything with her other than an abode? Or beyond even me: a young woman who wanted to be, let's say, an engineer, but who instead found herself barefoot and pregnant in a kitchen; a young woman who just wanted to live freely, but who is sequestered and maltreated by her insecure and brutal husband because her parents thought he would be a good spouse for her? You can argue your point, and I can see where you think it may be valid, but the fact is you cannot deny my reality, or the realities of the millions of young women out there whose voices were taken away from them when a choice was made *for* them, Mr. Ronald." I was aggravated. The day had not been a good one so far. I slammed the book closed, gathered my belongings, and excused myself to Mr. Ronald who was profusely apologizing for interrupting my morning and putting me in such a state.

I aimlessly walked around campus. I wistfully looked at the girls walking by, almost floating with their hair in the wind, free, insouciant, and I saw the deep gulf between us. No one would cut their clitoris out in the name of a vicious tradition or pick girls to marry at the bloom of their youth just like you would pick a ripe tomato in a grocery store; no one would dare question the presence or lack of a hymen on their wedding night. Of course, every person has their own woes, and I wondered what theirs were below the surface, but still I wanted to be saved from the unfairness of it all.

I heard a voice calling out my name. I recognized it right away.

"Hey! Aminatou from Guinea!" I looked back and saw him giving dap to a couple of other guys before he started running toward me. Oh god, I have been crying; are my eyes puffy? That was the first thought that entered my head as he approached. He remembered my name, and he had said it right.

"What's up, Amy?" He said when he got close and went in for a hug. I awkwardly hugged him back. He smelled of a masculine cologne. "How have you been?" he asked, looking at me with a big smile on his face.

"I am good, and you?" I stuttered.

"Same ol', same ol'. What are you up to?"

"Nothing really." We started walking side by side.

"Do you want to grab a bite?" he asked.

I checked the time on my phone. I still had about an hour free. "Sure, why not?" I told him.

"Alright! Let's get some pupusas!" He rubbed his hands together.

"Pupusas? What is that?" I asked him. He grinned mischievously.

"You will find out shortly!"

We walked and chatted on the way. It had been a rough morning for me, and I appreciated the sudden change of pace and turn of events.

"What are you studying?" I asked him.

"Mechanical engineering. I am in my third year. How about you?"

"I do not know yet; I am a freshman. I am thinking about accounting and finance."

"That's a good major." He extended his arm to stop me before crossing the street. "What made you choose that?"

"I want to go where the money is," I smiled. "I kind of like my Accounting 101 class, and I think I want to go into business after school."

"Okay, miss! I see you!" he laughed. He was wearing his cap backward, and he walked with assurance in his step.

We arrived at the restaurant. It was a small Salvadorian restaurant that had opened recently. The inside was very colorful and cheery. We took a seat at one of the tables. The atmosphere was welcoming, and Latin music flowed out of the speakers.

"Since it is your first time, let me order for you. Prepare yourself to have your taste buds rocked, young lady!" He was confident when he spoke, his voice was deep, and it brought some extra attractiveness to him. I shyly asked him questions about himself while we waited for our food. He was one of four boys in his family. He had been born in Columbia, Maryland, and was raised by his grandmother. He had done a semester abroad in Munich, Germany, the year before, and the trip opened his eyes. He wanted to travel the world; no one in his family had ever been outside of the United States. He was involved with several organizations on campus, and he loved trying new foods. What we ordered came right then. It was a platter of thick flatbread, stuffed with different ingredients like Enoch had requested.

"Did you put the pork ones to the side?" he asked the waiter.

"Yes, they are right here," the waiter said, pointing to one side of the platter.

"Okay great, we do not want Miss Aminatou eating the pork now!" he said, laughing. "Well, bon appétit!" I took a bite and was pleasantly surprised. It reminded me of the fatayas back home in some way. He took his turn asking me questions. I didn't know what was going on with me; I usually shied away from sharing details about my life, but I spilled everything to him by the time we had finished eating.

"Damn!" he said. "Too bad you are going to class; you need a stiff drink."

"I do not drink."

"Oh, is that also a religious thing, or do you just choose not to?"

"Both."

He was pensive for a moment, before saying, "You know, since you are fluent in French and some West African languages, you could apply to be a freelance interpreter. I know a company that hires people with your skills to provide translation at the hospital. You register in their database, and they call you when they are in need. You can take or decline the gig based on your availability. They pay well; it could be a few extra bucks for you." I said yes without hesitation. I would figure out how to work it into my already-packed schedule. I checked my phone, and I had only a few minutes left before class. We picked up our things and started dashing back toward the sociology building.

Later at the salon, my case was on the docket. I knew they had been talking about me right before I arrived because the salon went silent as soon as I walked in. The only sound you could hear was from the Nigerian movie on the television.

"You don't have to pretend, carry on!" I said, slightly annoyed. They all burst out laughing. Aunty Hassanatou had called Aunty Kadiatou just a few moments before to ask her to talk some sense into me, Salimata told me when I went behind the counter to drop my bag off.

"Amina, help Mireille out with the finishing. There is another customer coming in half an hour," Aunty Kadiatou said from the couch. I pulled a stool up to Mireille's station and started working on the braids in the back. It was a full minute before Ndeye said in her loud voice, "So, are you going to tell us what happened or what?"

"What is it to you?" I snapped back.

"Oooooh..." a couple of the girls jeered.

"Stop it!" Aunty Kadiatou interjected. "We will not have that here, and you should all learn to mind your own business and not to eavesdrop on people's conversations." Everyone focused on the television.

"Ah, ma chérie, en tous cas, we are here for you if you need us though," Bintou said gently after a while. I appreciatively nodded to her.

"This is the land of the free, oh! Nobody can tell you what to do," Ndeye's voice echoed again. "They do not understand the situation here. Times have changed. We women work, we pay our own bills, and we buy our own clothes, and we do not have to stay with someone if we do not want to!" She kissed her teeth. "If they start acting up, you kick them to the curb and get yourself a new man. There are plenty more fish in the sea."

"Yes honey, here we return men to their families, not the other way around!" Fanta chimed in. They all cackled.

"Shut up girl, you know you were returned to your family like a sack of potatoes," Mireille teased. They laughed harder.

"But who is the sack of potatoes now? He wishes he had me now. He is killing himself trying to get back in my house. Never happening!"

"You know what though? There should be a law." Amandine jumped into the conversation. "If you have to return me to my family after marrying me, you have the reset me to factory settings like my computer. Give me back my youth, those firm breasts, that tight body, my virginity—I want it all back!" she said, smacking her behind as she walked away. The whole room rolled in laughter. I joined in the banter. The atmosphere was back to normal. Aunty Kadiatou did not say anything to me. I had expected her to call me to the side at any moment during the whole afternoon, but she quietly sat on the couch, dozing off sometimes. Salimata walked with me to Popeyes when my shift's start time rolled around. She sat in one of the booths to finish her paper, and I gave her my free chicken meal.

Bouba was at home when I came back to the apartment. He was seated at the dinette table, eating a plate of leftover rice and beef stew.

"Hi," he said, acting normal. I said hello back and went to the kitchen to get some water. I observed him for an instant. The scraping of the plate drove me insane. Every time he scooped a spoonful of rice, the silverware hit the plate with a loud clinking noise. He then dragged the spoon around, gathering the rice and mixing it with the stew, hitting the plate and making a harsh scraping noise. When he finally lifted the spoon to his mouth, he chewed loudly and interminably before taking a big swig of his water, gulping it all down. It drove me crazy. I stood across the small dining table, staring, unable to drink my water while he kept scraping, lifting, chewing, and gulping, completely oblivious. I headed to the shower. I scrubbed the chicken smell off of me. When I was done, I closed the toilet lid and sat on it for a long time. I did not want to talk to him. All of a sudden, I could not stand him. I did not want to be in the same room with him. I remembered that I had not finished my assignments, so I walked out of the bathroom, picked up my book bag, and went to the bedroom. I settled on the bed with my folders around me and tuned out the world.

Chapter Fifteen

I saw Enoch more often on campus. We studied together at the library, ate more pupusas, and walked around campus talking about anything and everything. He sometimes rode the train with me and walked me to work. He usually turned around when we arrived a block away from the salon. He was extremely outgoing, optimistic, undefeated, and always in a good mood. I liked hanging out with him. Meanwhile, Bouba came home less and less. Aunty avoided my calls, and Uncle Abdul was evasive when I asked him about the divorce procedure. He repeated the same words as Aunty. My bind to Bouba was sacred, and he did not dare break it; besides, he was only my maternal uncle with not much say. It was so easy to hide behind that fact. I had absolutely no desire to talk to my paternal uncles, so Koto advised me to go see an imam. I woke up more often in the middle of the night in a cold sweat and laid wide awake, staring at the ceiling for the rest of the night.

There was no progress with my family in the following weeks, so I made an appointment to see an imam. I arrived at the Islamic center early in the afternoon after my classes. I took care to bring a scarf to cover my head. I was directed to a small room covered in rugs. I removed my shoes before entering and sat on a cushion on the floor. The imam walked in a few moments later and greeted me with a warm smile. He was younger than I thought he would be. I almost expected an older man to walk in, dressed in a large caftan, with a long beard and prayer beads glued to his fingers, but he wore a brown blazer with some khaki pants. His face was covered with a short-trimmed beard, and he wore glasses. "How are you today?" he asked me as he sat across from me.

"I am doing well, thank you."

"I am Imam Selim. What can I do for you today?"

I hesitated for a moment and could not form my words. He patiently waited, until I finally said, "I would like to divorce from my husband, and I am not sure how to properly do it. That is why I am here today to seek some counseling."

"Mmm...okay, I see," he murmured. He took a pause before continuing.

"Marriage is a solemn covenant in Islam and is meant to be forever. It is however permissible for couples who can no longer live with each other in harmony to resort to divorce. There is a misconstruction that Islam does not allow a woman the right to divorce her husband, but of course that is untrue. Unfortunately, there will always be people who spread misinformation in order to maintain power over the fairer sex, and this distortion is reinforced by social stigma and the barring of girls and women from Islamic education." He paused again for an instant, as if searching for his words. "As a woman, you can request a divorce from your husband for certain reasons. The thing which is prohibited is a wife seeking a divorce from her husband for no reason of the Shariah. Have you suffered physical, financial, or emotional harm from your husband? Has he been unfaithful? Or does he suffer from physical limitations such as impotence?"

Our case was not a clear black-and-white situation, so I explained to him in detail the circumstances in which we were married, what had transpired from it since I arrived in the United States, and the recent developments. He was meditative for a moment.

"You do not have any children, I assume?" he inquired.

"That is correct."

"Do you have any family here?"

"Just a distant aunt," I answered, shuddering at the idea of Aunty and Uncle being involved in this process.

"Well, based on what you have told me, I believe that your request is appropriate. If you are certain that there are no ways of mending it, and you decide that this is the way you would like to go, then you can petition for an Islamic divorce. There are steps to follow of course, and I will need to obtain your husband's contact information to set up a separate meeting with him." He took a moment to explain some things to me and informed me that the center offered marriage counseling services if we were interested. I listened politely and thanked him for the information when he was done. I pulled out a notebook, tore a sheet out of it, and scribbled Bouba's phone number and email on it.

"Could you please wait before contacting him? We need to talk first."

"Of course, not a problem." He handed me a business card with his information on it. "Feel free to reach out anytime. Are you a member of our center?"

"No, I am not," I responded.

"You should think about joining. We have a variety of programs and services that could be of interest to you."

"I will look into it, Imam." With that, we said our goodbyes, and I left.

A customer threw a drink at me that evening. He yelled things at me that I could not understand. I was shocked by what had happened. I stood still as the Fanta dripped off of me and onto the floor. "Why don't you go back to where you came from?!" he yelled before swinging the door behind him and disappearing into the night. Everyone was frozen in place. I saw a light flash before me, and my ears started drumming. I felt someone pull me by the arm and take me to the back. As I changed out of my uniform, I could not control the tears. I shook in anger. I wanted to walk out of the door right then, but I had to keep going. I could not afford to leave. Not yet. My situation was precarious. I was losing the roof over my head any day, I had a portion of school fees I was responsible for, and I wanted to save money in order to eventually sponsor Ousbi to come join me. I could not afford to leave yet. Chicken, beans and rice, and biscuits. Biscuits, and beans and rice, and fries, and chicken. They paraded in front of me, filled my days, but I had to push through. I missed home and I missed my family. My life in America was far from what I had imagined. I wished I could go back sometimes, but that was until I remembered the situation I left behind, and besides I couldn't possibly leave especially that I was now studying. I was a student in an American university. I had hope for a better future. I couldn't give up just because I encountered a few snags. I cried on the phone when I called Enoch that night, after I couldn't reach Fatima. He listened and gently comforted me. "We will find you something else, no need to worry." Somewhere during the conversation, he suggested something that I thought I misheard at first. I asked him to repeat it. "I am just saying that you could probably benefit from some therapy, with everything that has happened in your life and your current situation."

"There is nothing wrong with me!" I recoiled.

"Of course not, that is not what I am saying. Talking to a professional does not mean that something is wrong with you. I did it myself for chronic anxiety. I tried to solve it on my own but had to recognize at some point that I needed help. I used to be ashamed of it, but that was really silly."

"There is nothing wrong with me, Enoch!" I repeated, a little more forcibly.

"Okay, okay. All I am saying is that masking pain and anxiety is not the healthiest thing to do, and sometimes all you need is a professional ear." I wrapped up the call with him and went to sleep. I woke up again in the middle of the night in a cold sweat.

I sometimes looked at my life and wondered if everyone else's life was as warped as mine. What was the meaning of it all? I figured I would have to wait and find out. The conversation I had with Bouba was unextraordinary. We were both thinking the same thing, but neither of us wanted to be the one to say it out loud. We danced around it for a while before I flatly said it.

"I went to see an imam to inquire about a divorce procedure."

He looked up. He seemed surprised but did not say anything. I continued, "It is time to put an end to this; you and I both know it." He nodded. We sat silently for a moment.

He swallowed hard, then spoke. "What did the imam say?"

"That it is allowable based on what I explained to him, but he will need to speak with you. I gave him your contact information, so he may be calling you."

"Does your family know?"

"Yes, they do. I told them a while ago, but I was not seeing any evolution; that is why I went to see the imam."

"I understand," he said after a moment. He ran his hand over his head, looking preoccupied. "I have to figure things out with my family. Of course, that has nothing to do with you; I am just saying." I did not answer. "I am truly sorry for all this, Amina. It shouldn't have happened in the first place." He stood up and walked to the window.

"You do not have to leave. At least not right away. There is still a little time left on the lease; you can stay here while you figure out the next steps for you. I will help with the rent." There was a faint drop in my stomach. This was it—I would be on my own soon; there was no going back. I had always lived with someone and depended on someone to a certain extent. I panicked a little.

"You can keep the furniture if you wish." His voice brought me back.

The room fell silent for a few minutes. He stared out the window while I fiddled with the placemat on the table. I did not harbor any ill feelings toward him. The whole experience was trying, his plan lousy, but I was thankful for where I was, where he had helped me arrive in a short time. After a while, he turned around and broke the silence.

"In front of God, I ask you forgiveness for any harm I may have done to you," he said, looking straight at me.

"In front of God, I ask you forgiveness for any harm I may have done to you," I repeated back to him. We still had procedures to go through, but with those words, it was final. We had both acknowledged the end of the relationship and shared the parting words.

I felt tired and sick the following few days. I dragged myself to my classes, then to the salon, and finished the day at Popeyes. Aunty called me repeatedly, but it was my turn to avoid her calls. Bouba's family had probably reached out to her and Uncle about what was happening. After a few days, I pulled Salimata outside to talk privately.

"I have been feeling funny in this area," I said, making a waving motion around my lower body. "And I feel bloated and tired all the time."

"Oh, when did it start?"

"A few days ago," I told her.

"You may have to see a doctor. We'll need to make an appointment."

"At the hospital?" I asked her, a little worried.

"No, not at the hospital. Do you have a primary care doctor?"

I looked at her curiously.

"No," I finally answered. Have a doctor? I wanted to explain to her that where I came from, when you felt sick, you went to a dispensary and talked to whoever was there, and if it was really serious you went to one of the big hospitals, Donka or Ignace Deen. But how would she know?

"Hmm... you do not look unwell enough to warrant a trip to the emergency room. I am assuming you do not have insurance, so we will have to figure something out really quick, but don't worry, okay? I will look into it now," she said, gently rubbing my arm. We started heading back to the door when she stopped and said, "Oh, I know, let me call Planned Parenthood."

"Okay," I said, acting as if I knew what she was talking about. She was fumbling with her phone already.

"It looks like the closest one to us in in Silver Spring. That is where I go for birth control. Don't tell my mom!" She said, looking at me with a serious face before dialing the number.

"Hello, I was wondering if you take walk-ins?" She listened as someone spoke on the other side of the line before speaking again. "It is not for me, it is for my friend—she needs a well-woman visit with a doctor, and she does not have insurance." I looked at her, trying to make out what was going on the other side. "Tomorrow morning?" She looked at me inquisitively. I quickly did a mental rundown of my morning and nodded yes to her. "Okay, sounds good, we'll be there!" She hung up the phone. "Done. I will come with you." She smiled at me. My phone rang just then. It was Imam Selim. He wanted Bouba and I to come see him the next day.

The next morning, Salimata sat in the waiting room while I walked to the back with the nurse who murdered my name. We entered a small room, and she closed the door behind her. She checked my height, weight, temperature, and blood pressure before motioning me toward the exam table. She sat down on the chair, facing me, put her computer on her lap, and asked me for my name and date of birth before starting a series of questions about the reason for my visit, my last period, my medical history, my alcohol and drug use. She typed away studiously as I answered her questions.

"Are you sexually active?"

"Just once," I replied timidly.

"When was that?"

"Last year."

"Have you ever been checked for sexually transmitted diseases?"

"Yes, I was during my visa process last year."

"Okay, we offer free STD testing here. Would you like

to get tested since it has been a year?"

"Sure," I answered mechanically.

"When was your last pap test?" she asked next.

"What is that?" I asked her.

"Have you ever seen a gynecologist? Did you ever get a pelvic exam?" There was a pause before she said, "I guess that is a no," seeing how clueless I was.

"Do you feel safe at home?" I was surprised by the question but answered that I did.

"Good, we like to use the privacy of the exam room to ask this question. Whatever you tell me stays with me, okay?" I nodded. "And just for your information, if you ever feel you need to talk to someone about anything, just give us a call; there are professionals we can refer you to! Go ahead and get undressed, you can use that to cover up," she said, pointing to a folded paper square on the exam table. "The doctor will be in shortly." I started undressing and inelegantly laid the wrapper on me to cover my upper legs and private parts. How are you supposed to cover up with that? I could barely get it around me; how about the plumper women?

I waited awhile before there was an almost imperceptible knock on the door. The doctor was a short redheaded woman. She was very friendly and made me feel comfortable during my exam.

"Lay back and relax, you are going to feel some pressure," she warned me before she started the pelvic exam. We chatted throughout the exam, with me trying to ignore the fact that someone's head was between my spread legs, inspecting my vajayjay.

"Have you been stressed recently?" she asked me.

"I don't think so," I lied.

"The nurse told me you have not been feeling well, but other than this discomfort in your private area, you do not have any other symptoms?"

"Correct."

"Well, it is possible you are suffering from fatigue, and you may be developing a little yeast infection."

"What?" I asked her. "I do not understand what that means."

"A yeast infection can be caused by candida overgrowth. It can stem from a number of factors. If you are under stress for a prolonged period of time, the body could begin to produce increased levels of cortisol. It is a hormone that can weaken the immune system and simultaneously cause high levels of blood sugar. Yeast feeds off sugar, and it allows the candida to grow faster than normal. I am going to look at this culture in detail, but I am more than certain that it is yeast. Not to worry, however; I am going to prescribe you some Diflucan, and it should clear up in no time. I will be right back!" And her white coat disappeared behind the door.

Chapter Sixteen

I stopped by the pharmacy on my way to see Imam Selim. I was appalled at the price of that one miniscule pill, but I needed it, so I reluctantly paid and took it right there. Bouba was already seated with the iman in the small room when I arrived. We greeted each other before Imam Selim went over some procedures, including the return of the dowry, which Bouba declined. The situation was a bit unusual as the families were usually present, but given the circumstances, we could overrule it. We engaged with each other for almost a half hour before

Imam Selim confirmed one last time if I still wanted a divorce. I confirmed.

"Then you must officially ask for it," he said softly.

I turned toward Bouba and solemnly said, "I am asking you for a divorce."

"And I give it to you," he answered in an equally solemn way. I tuned out the following part until the imam's voice registered in a slightly higher pitch.

"That is it, then! You will still have to file for a civil procedure back in your country of origin since that is where you were married officially, but we are done here. One last note, however, and this is for you," he said, looking at me. "As a divorced woman, you are not permitted to remarry during the period of the iddah, which is three menstrual cycles or three months." I acquiesced, thinking that it was far from being a concern. "Also, as a divorced woman, you could engage in relationships through mutah before deciding if you want to remarry another man. This applies to both of you. I bring it up because you are both young, and you may be faced with some situations that clash with your religion."

"What is that, Imam?" I asked. He shifted in his seat and adjusted his glasses before answering.

"It is an unusual and touchy subject, but a mutah is essentially a temporary marriage used in the same way as a permanent marriage in order to make a man and woman halal to each other. Of course, there are rules to abide by, but in essence, it is a contract that can be verbal or written. The union can last for a few hours, days, months, or however long the involved parties wish for, and when the contract ends, so does the marriage." He paused while I wrapped my head around what he was saying. I looked at Bouba, and he looked equally surprised. Imam Selim continued, "It is very informal and is accomplished with a few recited words and an agreed-upon dowry from the man to the woman; it does not have to be fancy, just a simple gift could do it. It can be done with or without witnesses. In your case, Amina, since you have already been married once, you would not need a father's permission."

"Wow!" The word escaped my mouth before I realized it. Imam Selim smiled slightly.

"Many religious leaders would not bring this up; in fact, many actually reject it, but the truth is, times have changed, and things can get a little murky with the new generations, so this is a way of balancing religious beliefs with modern Western lifestyle. It is just something I would like you to keep in mind."

I was in shock. How had I never heard of this? I was not sure how I felt about it, however. It was two extremes for the woman. She could either be married, or she could be a rented woman because that was what it came down to—a time-constricted relationship in exchange for a sum or a gift. I couldn't wait to tell Fatima, Salimata, and Enoch and to hear their thoughts about it, but what mattered at the moment was that I was free. *Free*. I said the word to myself, and I could not believe it; it felt odd. I called off work that evening and went straight back to the apartment after Bouba and I parted ways, both physically and symbolically.

I sat on the couch, then at the dinette, then back on the couch. I listened to the silence and the sound of my heart flutter. I was overwhelmed by a feeling of dread. I had unloaded one heavy weight from my shoulders, but another one was creeping up, pushing me down, paralyzing me and crushing my chest. I heavily dragged myself to bed and tucked my body under the covers. I did not get up the next morning when my alarm went off or when my phone rang over a dozen times. I switched it off and turned to face the wall. A loud banging on the door brought me out of my slumber. I looked around, disoriented, unsure of how long I had been in bed. I covered my head with the covers, but the banging would not stop, so I eventually hauled myself to the door.

"Who is it?"

"Open the door, Amina!" I heard Salimata's voice say firmly. I unlocked the door and pulled it slightly open. In the hallway, Salimata was standing next to Aunty Kadiatou, a worried look on both their faces.

"We have called you a thousand times, and it keeps going to voicemail!" Salimata said, pushing me out of the way and walking into the apartment. "What is going on?"

"Nothing," I grumbled and slumped in the couch. Aunty Kadiatou had also walked in and was scrutinizing me as she clutched her purse. "Open the blinds, Sali," she said as she sat next to me. The light blinded me.

"What is wrong? You had us worried sick, Amina," Aunty Kadiatou said softly. I tried to protest that nothing was wrong, but what came out was a strange sound, a sob, maybe, as I fell on her shoulder.

"I am scared," I managed to mouth in between gurgling and crying noises. She gently rubbed my back.

"What are you scared of?" Salimata sounded off. "Scared because you are actually not married anymore? Because you are going to be your own person? You should be celebrating; there are worse problems to have!"

"Shush, Sali!" Aunty Kadiatou reprimanded her. "It will be okay; it will be okay..." She continued rubbing my back. Salimata sat on the other side of me, shifting the balance on the couch, and took my hand. I am not sure how long we stayed there in silence, but that is all that I needed, their comforting presence and a shoulder to lean on.

Spring arrived with its pleasant florid smell, delicate dawn mist, and budding flowers. I had weathered the storm. I survived the dark days, the days of doubt, the days of questioning my decision. I survived the admonishing, the shaming, the acrimonious calls from both my family and Bouba's. Being a pariah wasn't so bad after all. I had my family, the one I had chosen, holding me up and supporting me through it all. After much insisting from Enoch, I finally started seeing a friend. He suggested I call her "a friend" because "mental health professional" rubbed me the wrong way. I spent even more time with Enoch. I was utterly annoyed at how he was always on my mind lately. His know-it-all attitude irked me at times, but whenever he looked at me, something fuzzy swirled in me.

"Go for it—you like him, girl. I don't know why you are even pretending," Fatima laughed. "You need to come out of your own head and pull that stick out of your you-know-what...it would do you some good." She now had a Canadian boyfriend, but it was a secret between us as her family could not find out. Her mother had started giving out her number to young Guinean men who were also studying in Canada or the United States, hoping that Fatima could find a husband among them. Her parents wanted her to get married as soon as possible while she was still young, and therefore by their own account, suitable and desirable for marriage. Fatima was always startled to receive phone calls from random numbers with men on the other side of the line clumsily explaining how they got her contact. We often laughed about it even though we knew deep down that she would have to stop ignoring it at some point.

Enoch lived in an apartment complex right outside of campus. "Do people not cook here?" I asked him once, genuinely curious. He looked at me with a raised eyebrow.

"Well, the hallway does not smell like food. In fact, there is a complete absence of smell," I quickly explained. He laughed. "Well, I see you live in an immigrant building!" He laughed even harder. "No, I am kidding...a little." He caught his breath. "It is mostly students living here, and we live on pizza, noodles, and tacos. In fact, let me order us a pizza." He pulled out his phone. We were about to study for our finals and the library was packed, so he had suggested we walk back to his apartment since his roommate was also at the library.

"What do you mean by immigrant building earlier? That sounds wrong."

"Come on, lighten up, I am just kidding!" He nudged me. "But there is a reason I said that. You know that I have many international friends, and it just happens that whenever I visit them, there is always a delicious smell in the hallways. We never had that in all of the places I lived growing up. Maybe it is because we cook less and eat out more. I do not say it in a demeaning way, but most immigrants tend to live in the same areas and buildings, so you see my logic here?"

"Well there is a reason for that, too—people tend to want to be where their family or friends are. I don't see what is wrong with that!"

"I am not saying that anything is wrong with it...oh, forget it! Come on in!" I realized I was standing at the door. I pushed the pile of things on the packed coffee table to the side to make space for my books. Enoch brought us some chips to snack on while we waited for the pizza.

We must have stayed there for hours because when I looked up at some point, it was dark outside. I had used a few of my paid-time-off days to study for my finals. Enoch let out a loud sigh and let his head fall against the back of the sofa. His head was right there, inches away from mine. I did not know what got into me, but before I knew it, I had leaned over to kiss him. He kissed me back and shifted to bring me in closer. I came up for air after a while. I did not know what this was, but I was overcome with strange sensations of want and need, feelings that I had never experienced before. Whatever it was, I did not want it to stop, so I pushed all thoughts to the back of my head. His hands were moving all over my body, fumbling to remove my shirt. I pulled back for a second. I had never been naked in front of any man other than Bouba, and even then, I had been under the shield of the covers; but Enoch...his eyes were looking at me intently, and I could almost feel his gaze like a soft burn on my skin.

"I have never...I am..." I stumbled on my words.

"It's okay. You are overthinking. You are beautiful," he said as he put his hand on the back of my head and pulled me back in for a kiss. We removed each other's clothes clumsily. I stared at him when he was naked and standing in front of me in all his splendor. Handsome, strong, manly. I shivered unintentionally. I did not care about anything anymore at that moment. All that mattered was this. Having him. I shocked myself with my overwhelming desire for him and arched against him when he slowly let his body fall over me as he gazed down at me, and we let ourselves go in the dance of lust.

Hours later, when I lay in bed back in my room, I thought I had imagined it, but I knew it had been real as my skin still singed, and my belly whirred. "Fireworks, Fatima, it was like fireworks!" I giggled on the phone. I could not wait until morning to call her.

"Details!!" she screamed in the phone, and I went on to recount the evening to her.

"Did you use protection?" she asked after I was done.

"Of course!"

"Oh good! You probably need to get on birth control, too. You can never be too safe."

"I will look into it." I paused for a moment. "Fatima, I did not know a body, *my* body, could experience that. How was that even possible? Isn't excision supposed to keep you from having pleasure?"

"Stop being dumb, Mina! You know damn well that is not true. Butchering a woman's privates and subjecting women to unthinkable pain is the only thing that that screwed-up thing accomplishes."

A small but significant part of me had been cut out of me, but they had lost, and I had won, I thought with an impish smile on my face. I knew that many were not as lucky. I had had a piece of my clitoris removed, but some girls were subjected to infibulation, which involved narrowing the vaginal opening by cutting, repositioning, and stitching the labia; and sometimes they underwent the removal of both the clitoris and the labia minora, which in fact succeeded at robbing them of having any kind of sexual life for the rest of their existence—and I say existence because living a life without being able to effectively enjoy the part that is as primordial to a human's well-being as sleeping and eating is in fact just existing. I had felt rage toward my Aunty Hawa, as well as the rest of the family who had been aware of it, for letting it happen. I had been convinced that this part of my life had been taken away from me when all I had experienced with Bouba was friction and pain, not pleasure. Turned out, that just had to do with my lack of yearning for him. Luck, pure luck—I got lucky, I thought to myself. They tried to control me and strip me of sexual desire and enjoyment, something I had a right to as much as any man, but at that they had failed because desire, I did have; enjoyment, I did partake in; orgasm, I did experience.

"So, you had an orgasm?" Fatima inquired and pulled me out of my thoughts.

"Yes giiirl...and it was glorious!" And we both burst out in laughter.

The following couple of weeks were some of the most exhilarating and happiest times I had known. We spent hours studying in secluded corners of the library, stealing kisses and touches. I felt bad because I dropped my regular study group, but the guilt was soon replaced by anticipation, longing. After our exams, we spent a couple of stolen hours in his apartment, where our bodies were entangled, occasionally leaving to walk down the street to pick up food while holding hands before we both went to work. I laughed a lot, had an extra pep in my step, and felt giddy and cheerful. So, this was what all the fuss was about.

"If you become divorced, you will become a pariah. Is that what you want?" Aunty's words resonated in my head. Well, if this was what it felt like, then yes, I was happy to be a pariah. I dreaded the day we would see each other face to face, but right then, it did not matter, and I pushed it back, far and tucked away in the back of my head. I did not want anything raining down on my parade, as the Americans said. Bouba had called a couple of times to check on me, and we talked briefly and said goodbye, both of us relieved to hang up the phone. Enoch suggested I move into his apartment because his roommate would be moving out soon. I considered it, but it did not feel right. Seeing him made my stomach flutter, made my days instantly brighter, and made me feel giddier; but still, it did not feel right. I knew, however, that I had to leave Bouba's apartment. It was not mine, it had never felt mine, and I would not truly break the chains until I left it. I had to leave. I knew that it wouldn't be a field trip, but it was necessary. I needed to do it for me, to prove to myself that I could do it, that I could truly be independent, truly be my own person. I visited some apartments, but it seemed like the more I searched, the shoddier they became. Apparently, in the Washington, DC, area, all my budget and almost-nonexistent credit history could afford me was pest-infested housing in questionable neighborhoods, with peeling paint and stains on the ceilings. I was starting to despair but hoped that I would find that perfect place with the perfect price tag. Eventually. I picked up more hours at work and promptly accepted whenever I received a call to interpret at the hospital.

Salimata surprised me. I asked her again to make sure I had heard her right.

"Let's move in together!" she repeated excitedly. I gasped.

"I thought you were going to stay at home to save for your Africa trip and your first condo!"

"Yes, but situations change. You are my girl now, my homie. Let's do it. Mom will co-sign for us."

"You mean she is already onboard?!" I almost screamed.

"Girl, didn't I just tell you she will co-sign?" We both screamed.

We moved a couple of weeks later. I stood at the threshold of Bouba's apartment and scanned the room one last time. Farewell. All my life, I had waited to live. Waited for something astounding to happen, something that would catapult me to the next level and allow me to finally live my life. That something never came. It took me long enough to grasp the idea that I had to create it myself. As agonizing and uneasy as it was, I sensed the crucial need to reach deep within my fears and angst to create my own path toward normalcy again. At least, my idea of what normalcy was. The metaphorical roof was off, the shelter was gone. It was now me, just me. It was time to be just me. To be Amina. Amina minus the husband. Amina minus the male figure hovering over her. The girl whose world crumbled from underneath her and fell into an abyss of uncertainty, but who crawled her way out of it. Aminatou who made good and questionable decisions, but who came out at the other end, still standing. I would forever be the woman who left her husband, who disobeyed and brought dishonor to her family. But I chose to see it as being the woman who stood up for herself. The one who challenged the patriarchy and dared to break free of a life of subjugation. My flame was starting to glisten. I hoped Neneh was proud of me.

www.ingramcontent.com/pod-product-compliance
Lightning Source LLC
Chambersburg PA
CBHW022048240626
47154CB00007B/2610

* 9 781735 645605 *